LAURIE'S SONG

"As a matter of fact," Skip said, "I think I've got a rough idea of how it's going to sound already. Want to hear it?"

I was so beside myself with joy, I could only nod my head, feeling the flush creep up and across my cheekbones as he started singing in a low husky voice. I'd written the song just for him, and now he was singing it...just for me.

Laurie's Song

Suzanne Rand

BANTAM BOOKS
Toronto · New York · London · Sydney

RL 5, IL age 11 and up

LAURIE'S SONG
A Bantam Book/September 1981

Cover photo by Pat Hill

ISBN 0-553-20327-4

Published simultaneously in the United States and Canada

Bantam Books are published by Bantam Books, Inc. Its trade-
mark, consisting of the words "Bantam Books" and the por-
trayal of a bantam is Registered in U.S. Patent and Trademark
Office and in other countries. Marca Registrada. Bantam
Books, Inc., 666 Fifth Avenue, New York, New York 10103.

Printed and bound in Great Britain by
Cox & Wyman Ltd, Reading

Chapter One

Have you ever thought sometimes that it's more fun to imagine things than to actually do them? I have, and that's the first thing I thought of when I heard the dull, flat buzz of my little white alarm clock telling me it was seven o'clock and time to wake up and get dressed for my first day at Seven Oaks Senior High School. All summer long I'd dreamed about this day, but now that it was finally here, I wished it had remained a dream.

In my fantasies about high school, handsome boys chased me down long green corridors. They begged, "Please, Laurie, promise you'll go to the Soph Hop with me!" Teachers applauded me in front of the whole class, announcing, "Laurie Adams, that's the most original poem I've heard since Edna St. Vincent Millay." The most popular girls in the school, juniors and seniors as well as sophomores, insisted they'd cancel their slumber parties and picnics if I couldn't come. "It just wouldn't be the same without you, Laurie," they'd tell me.

But that morning the real Laurie Adams woke up feeling cold and clammy. I had a funny tightness in my chest. Maybe I was coming down with the flu.

I shut off the alarm, threw back the white chenille bedspread, and propped my pillow against the brass headboard. I sat up and studied the lace edging on the hem of my white nightgown as if I'd never seen it before. I wondered if I should tell Mom I was sick and had to stay in bed all day.

But I knew that even if I had pneumonia, I couldn't stay home. The only thing worse than the first day of high school would be missing it. I sighed, promising myself I'd get out of bed in just five more minutes.

Deep down inside, I knew I wasn't really sick— just scared. For a second I imagined myself showing up at Seven Oaks High tomorrow with a note to the principal in my mother's small, precise handwriting: *Please excuse my daughter Laurie from being absent on the first day of school. She was too scared to come.*

That made me feel so silly I jumped out of bed. As I headed toward the bathroom, I noticed the wooden plaque I'd woodburned in eighth grade art class. "Today is the first day of the rest of your life," it read. The words had never seemed truer.

This *was* the first day of the rest of my life. I was a new person, and it seemed almost funny that nothing else had changed. My room looked the same as always with its twin beds and fluffy rose shag rug and the white-painted bookcases that I'd helped Dad build. A Wesley Junior High School green-and-white pennant was tacked on the bulletin board over my desk. The only thing different was me. I was now a high-school student.

Why didn't I feel happier about it? I wondered as I stood under the shower in the little white-tiled bathroom next to my room. While I'd been waiting for summer to end so I could start school at Seven Oaks, I'd never thought that I might end up feeling so nervous. I couldn't remember feeling so jumpy since the summer I was nine years old.

That was when I was supposed to go to sleepaway camp for the first time. Didi Callahan had gone to Camp Rustic Pines the year before and was really excited about going again. Since whatever Didi did I wanted to do more than anything, I hadn't given my parents a moment's peace until they'd agreed that I could go away to camp with her.

The only problem was, after Mom had sent in the forms I started feeling scared about the idea of being away from home for a full month. I didn't dare confess this to anyone though—not even to Didi.

Even back then, Didi had seemed older and more sure of herself than I. When I'd asked her in a shaky voice if she didn't feel funny being so far away from home for such a long time, she had screwed up her pretty face, rolled her eyes, and tossed her strawberry blond curls as if I'd asked the dumbest question in the world.

"Feel funny about what, Laurie? Don't be such a baby! There're counselors and other kids all over the place. What's the matter? Are you afraid to go to bed if your mommy isn't there to tuck you in?"

I looked down so she wouldn't see the tears that had filled my eyes at being called a baby. "Of course not, dopey!" I lied. "I—I just wondered if you ever felt weird being by yourself so far away."

I was sure *I* would feel lonely and scared. I wished I'd never talked my parents into letting me go. Imagine my relief when the camp sent my parents a letter saying it was all filled up for that summer. No one ever knew my tears were tears of joy, not sadness. Now I could just think about the fun I would have had—instead of having to go there and be miserable.

I'd been saved from sleepaway camp, but nothing would save me from high school. I stepped out of the shower stall and wrapped myself in one of the oversized deep purple bath-sheets Mom and Dad had given me for my fifteenth birthday in January.

It wasn't just that the juniors and seniors and the school building would be new to me. Seven Oaks High School was the biggest school in the district, and kids from two other junior highs as well as those from Wesley would be there. That meant there would be all sorts of strange boys in my classes. And that really scared me.

You see, I'd never even had a real date. Sure, I'd gone to dances and parties in junior high, but they were events where boys had *had* to bring girls, so one of them figured he may as well ask me. I wasn't sure what going on a real date felt like, but I knew it wouldn't be the same as those forced dates. I was dying to have some guy ask me to go to the movies or for a burger and shake because he wanted to get to know *me*. But I couldn't imagine what I would do if someone actually did. I couldn't figure out what I'd talk about, either. It was like sleepaway camp. I wanted it so badly and was so scared at the same time that I got a knot in my stomach just thinking about it.

That's partly why I was so on edge about starting high school. I'd heard a lot of stories about girls who made bad first impressions and spent the rest of their time until graduation crying in their bedrooms while other girls had dates for dances and football games. I was terrified I might turn out to be one of those girls. Even though most of the stories sounded made up or exaggerated—like one Ellie Denman had told me in eighth grade about some girl who burped in class the first week of high school and was ignored until she went to college—I was still scared I'd do something awful to make me dateless for the rest of high school.

Trying to get dressed didn't soothe my raw nerve endings. I felt as if I were two different people. One me looked at the green-and-yellow plaid shirtwaist that I'd planned on wearing today and said, "Yes, that's the right kind of dress to wear for the first day of school." The other me laughed scornfully. "Oh, Laurie, you're going to look so dowdy. Like someone's mother on the way to a PTA meeting."

So no sooner had I put on the shirtwaist than I ripped it off. I flung it across my bed. By the time I'd dressed in a brown skirt and tan sweater, I was just as miserable. I looked all right, but the sweater was wool and made me perspire. If I went to school in seventy-four-degree heat dressed like that, I'd probably faint in the hallway and be ruined for sure.

I had just pulled off my blue jeans, which I'd decided were too sloppy, when Mom yelled from downstairs, "Laurie, your breakfast's on the table. You don't want to be late!"

No, I don't want to be late, I thought grimly, *I don't want to go at all!* Standing numbly in the middle of the room in just my underwear, I caught sight of my flushed face and bedraggled hair in the mirror. I wanted to scream. How was I going to show up at school looking calm and collected?

"Calm down," I whispered out loud. "Calm down and forget about clothes for five minutes."

But putting on my makeup made me just as unhappy. I looked too pale. My suntan had faded. So I put on gobs of my favorite coral blusher; I looked like I was running a fever. I tried to get the blusher off, and I rubbed at my face with a tissue until my skin felt raw. I couldn't tell if my cheeks were red from the blush or from scrubbing away at them.

When I went to put on mascara, my hand shook and the wand smeared thick brown goo on my right temple. I had to blot my lipstick three times until it didn't look too caked and glaring. By the time I was done, no one would have guessed I even had makeup on. There was more makeup on the wad of soiled tissues on the dresser than on my face.

Who'll notice anyway? I wondered, getting a sick sort of satisfaction from torturing myself. Ordinary old Laurie Adams, not plain but not pretty. Just medium—medium-tall, medium-figured, with medium-brown, medium-long hair.

"Be thankful you don't have ears that stick out or an ugly nose or crooked teeth," my mother had told me once when I was moaning about not being special looking. I guess I was lucky to be a five instead of a zero, but that still didn't make up for not being a ten, not in my book.

"Laurie!" Mom called again. This time her voice had that sharp little edge that it gets when she's starting to get angry or losing patience.

"I'll be right down!" I yelled, so fed up with myself by then that I threw on the first outfit I saw that I'd at least be comfortable wearing. My jeans skirt, Hawaiian print multi-colored blouse, and beaded moccasins weren't the most sensational things in my closet, but at least I'd feel like me in them, not like someone in disguise. I grabbed my notebooks and rushed from the room before I had a chance to change my mind.

Chapter Two

"Say hello to Didi," Mom called as I swung the front door open and hurried down the fieldstone path to the sidewalk. "And have a wonderful day!"

"Have fun at the hospital!" I yelled back cheerfully. I wondered if Mom could guess how much I'd rather be doing volunteer work with her than heading for the bus stop to catch the bus that would deliver me like a prisoner to the three-story building two miles away.

"Say hello to Didi," I mimicked under my breath as I turned off the path onto Oaktree Lane. I didn't dare look back at the familiar gray frame house because I was afraid I'd run inside and never come out again.

Mom had taken it for granted that Didi would be taking the bus with me today. Well, I'd taken it for granted, too, until I'd talked to Didi on the phone last night. After that conversation, however, I wondered if I could ever take anything for granted about Didi again.

When I turned the corner onto Maple Drive, I almost expected to see her waiting for me on her front porch to tell me she'd only been kidding about going to school with Wes and Coreen. But the porch was empty.

Didi had spent the whole summer at her grandmother's in Denver, and I had expected her to come over and suffer with me last night. So I felt as shocked as if she'd thrown a bucket of cold water on me when she had called and offhandedly remarked she was spending the night at home hanging out with her sister Coreen.

"She got all these great new albums while I was away. She said I can listen to them with her tonight. Mom and Dad say she can't go out with Wes since school starts tomorrow, and she's real down about being stuck here."

I almost said, "What about me being stuck *here*?" But I didn't want to sound depressed, so I just asked, "Since when do you have to stay in with Coreen? I thought you couldn't stand being around her."

"Coreen's all right, and she *is* my sister, Laurie," she answered in the kind of voice that meant "so drop it."

"Well, she might be your sister, but I'm your best friend. Besides, I wanted to show you some of the poems I wrote over the summer and see what you thought of them."

I heard Didi sigh, and when she spoke, her voice was thick with boredom. She spoke to me slowly and carefully, the way someone speaks to a child who isn't too bright.

"Laurie," she said, dragging my name out like molasses, "who wants to spend their last night of freedom reading, for goodness' sake? And, you know, it's silly to have best friends in high school."

"Since when did you hate to read my poems?" I asked. "You never thought they were dumb before. I suppose now that you think best friends are silly to have, you don't care about being on the honor roll anymore, either. Right?"

She didn't say anything.

"Well?" I asked. "Who says it's silly to have best friends?"

"Lots of people," she said angrily. "Coreen says all her friends are her friends equally. And she also says that nobody studies too hard at Seven Oaks."

"Coreen says!" My cheeks felt hot, and my heart was like a bowling ball caught in my chest. When I finally found my voice, it sounded high and squeaky and not like me at all. "Didi, I can't believe you pay attention to what Coreen says. Are you trying to tell me you don't want to be my best friend anymore or ever read a book or do well in school because of Coreen? I mean, what does Coreen know about anything? How can you even listen to someone whose biggest dreams in life are to be a beautician and marry Wes Kramer and who thinks *War and Peace* is the name of an English punk band?"

She laughed at that. Even though I hadn't been making a joke, I laughed with her. The constriction in my chest loosened up a bit now that I saw Didi didn't really mean anything about our not being friends and that she was just repeating dumb stuff Coreen had told her.

But at the end of the conversation, Didi really threw me. "I'll stop for you on the way to the bus stop," I said, not making it a question since we always went to school together.

But there was a long pause, and then Didi said in a funny little voice, "Ummm—not tomorrow, Laurie. Wes and Coreen said they'd give me a ride."

I guess it bothered her that I didn't answer. Maybe she knew how hurt I was feeling, and she didn't like the way that made *her* feel because she sounded pretty strange when she said loudly, "I mean, we can't always do everything together, Laurie!"

"You don't have to yell at me, Didi. It's not like *I'm* doing something rotten to *you.*"

"Look, let's not fight about it, Laurie. I'm still your best friend." She sounded like she meant it. "I'll save you a place in the cafeteria, all right?"

"Okay. Sure. See you at lunch." I knew my voice had gone small and cold, but I couldn't help it. At the same time, I couldn't blame Didi all that much for wanting to show up for the first day of school with Wes and Coreen. Even if they were dodos in a lot of ways, Wes was the star fullback on the football team and Coreen was a cheerleader. They were good people to be seen with. Still, I didn't think it was fair for Didi just to dump me that way. I didn't think it was fair at all.

That's why I was plodding up the street alone now, clutching my notebooks to my chest and ducking my head down as if it were cold and windy instead of sunny and warm. I told myself that if I didn't look up until I got to the bus stop, when I did, someone I knew would be there. It's an old game I've played when I've wanted something real bad. It's sort of like casting a magic spell. If I pretend something doesn't exist or that I don't want it, I will get it.

Since this little trick almost always failed, you'd have thought I would have stopped doing it. But at least it made me feel better.

I was so busy trying *not* to look at the bus stop and see who was waiting there that I forgot to look for traffic as I stepped off the curb. When a blaring car horn ripped into my ears, I jumped back so fast I almost lost my balance. I was so sure I was about to be run down that I could hear the thumping of my heart.

"Eyes up, beautiful!" Why, the dirty white Chevy hadn't even come close to hitting me! I tried to glare as it crawled by me, going only about twenty miles an hour, but I was still too shaken to look anything but dazed.

Then I got a brief glimpse of the boy who was driving, and my legs turned to jelly. I saw tanned, high cheekbones and a mop of blondish curls. Then he was gone, leaving behind a cloud of exhaust fumes as he sped up and spun away. Even if he had given me the biggest scare of my life, he was gorgeous—I didn't have to see him full-face to know that! I was shaking slightly as I crossed the street. Well, who wouldn't be trembling if they'd almost been killed by some crazy kid, I asked myself. But I didn't feel as mad as I thought I should. I kept seeing that cloud of golden curls shining against the whiteness of the car. I kept hearing the laugh in his voice when he'd yelled, "Beautiful." I knew he was only teasing, making fun of me for not watching where I was going. But I couldn't help feeling sort of glowy inside as I replayed his words over and over again in my head.

I was so wrapped up in these thoughts that before I knew it I was at the bus stop. Janie Elkins was there, so my magic spell had worked. I wouldn't be riding the school bus alone in a sea of total strangers. The kids who were standing there all looked at me as I walked up, but Janie was the only one I knew.

"Are you all right, Laurie?" Janie asked. Beneath her thick fringe of short, dark bangs, her forehead wrinkled, and her eyes looked worried. "The way some people drive! He could have killed you!"

"No, no, I'm all right, really." I could feel my ears growing hot. I knew I was blushing under the stares of the other kids. "It's my fault for not paying attention."

"Well, I still think it was a dumb thing for him to do," Janie said. She sounded vaguely puzzled, as if she didn't understand why I wasn't more upset about it.

"Do you know who he was?" I asked, trying not to let my interest show in my voice.

She shook her head. "Someone who shouldn't be driving around, that's for sure."

I changed the subject. "Speaking of cars, how come you're taking the bus instead of catching a ride with your brother?"

"Football. Bob's been going to practice at dawn

every day with some of the other guys," she explained proudly. For a minute I wished I were Janie, with a big brother who was a senior, president of student council, and a star athlete. "Every fall Bob changes from my mild-mannered brother into Super Jock. He eats, sleeps, and breathes football."

I couldn't think of anything else to say about Bob Elkins, whom I didn't even know. I just stood jiggling my notebooks against my hip and scuffing the toe of my moc along the grass bordering the sidewalk. I wished that I could come up with something interesting to say to Janie.

I didn't know her very well, even though she always went out of her way to be friendly and had usually picked me for her team whenever she was a field hockey captain in gym class. I guess I'd always thought of Janie as being a little bit out of my league and didn't expect her to want to be close friends with me.

Like her brother Bob, Janie was kind of an all-around kid: athletic, pretty smart, cute in a pixieish sort of way, and destined to be popular, no matter what. I thought it was only natural that she'd pick her closest friends from the girls who were as well liked as she was. Even now, when she seemed to really want to be with me, I told myself that if any of those girls had been at the bus stop, Janie probably would have ignored me.

At Wesley, I'd thought of myself as part of the second-string clique, and I'd be happy enough to be in the same place at Seven Oaks. Considering how much I just sort of quietly hung out on the fringes, trying not to call much attention to myself, I guess it was strange I was as popular as I was.

I was so convinced that Janie Elkins thought I was dull and couldn't think of anything to say at all. But if I'd said what was on my mind, it would have been "Boy, am I glad to see you're wearing a jeans skirt almost like mine. If someone like you is wearing one, it must be okay." Only if I did, she really would have thought I had a screw loose!

"Here comes the jail wagon!" some boy yelled. Sure enough, an old yellow-orange bus was trundling around the corner a block away.

His remark was the signal for everyone to start groaning and hollering. Did everyone really hate school that much? I wondered. Or, like me, were they excited about starting high school but didn't want to show it in case someone laughed at them?

On the ride to school, I felt too queasy to talk to Janie, so I just stared out the window, my heart beating faster at each familiar signpost that was taking us closer to the school. I couldn't even tell if the other kids on the bus were as hyped up as I was. I heard one boy groan loudly from someplace in back of me. "Why did I have to get old man Lester for biology? I hear he's the worst!"

"No way, Burnett!" another voice I didn't recognize answered back. "*You're* the worst! Pity poor Mr. Lester if he's got to try to teach you anything this year."

"Hey, Susie, wanna meet me for a Coke after school?" a boy shouted.

When I heard a girl casually reply, "Sure, I'll see you at the front door after classes," I felt more out of it than ever. I was sure these kids were only sophomores, since every kid in our part of California somehow managed to scrape together money for a car by the time they were sixteen. And yet they thought nothing of making dates at the top of their lungs in front of a whole busload of people! Suddenly everyone's yelling and laughing was getting on my nerves, reminding me more and more that I didn't know how to belong. Even Janie seemed to have given up on me—maybe because I sat there so silently. She was still by my side but talking so quietly to the girl across the aisle that I couldn't even hear what they were saying.

Everyone got very quiet when the bus pulled into the black asphalt parking lot behind Seven Oaks. Maybe they're as scared as I am, after all, I thought in amazement. On the other side of the lot, the sun was beaming down on the short grass of the athletic field, and I could see a couple of guys in the school's gold and blue athletic jerseys trudging toward the back doors. Kids were milling around in little groups all over the parking lot, leaning against cars or sitting on the hoods. They waved and called to other kids as they arrived. I hoped that maybe on the first day of school next year, I'd be one of those kids, noisy and confident instead of shy and out of place.

I was wondering if it would look too pushy if I latched onto Janie and the other girl as they walked to the building. As I was working on building myself up to ask casually, "Okay if I go along with you?" I heard Didi's high-pitched voice calling my name. I turned around to look for her.

If I had any pride, I told myself, *I'd ignore her and walk away by myself.* But even as I told myself that, I was heading across the parking lot to meet her.

Chapter Three

"Laurie Adams! I can't believe you're wearing that ratty old skirt on the first day of school!" Didi groaned and widened her already huge green eyes. I noticed that her eyes looked even bigger than usual because she'd used bright, leaf-green eye shadow on her eyelids and a lot of mascara on her lashes.

"I like this outfit," I said stubbornly, biting my tongue to stop from adding that Janie Elkins was wearing a jeans skirt, too.

"Oh, it's great, real great," she said, tossing her short curls around to make the point in case I'd missed the sarcasm dripping from each word. Then she curled her lip and added, "It's exactly what I'd wear if I were starting sixth grade today."

"Very funny. At least I don't look like I'm on my way to a cocktail party! C'mon, let's go inside—or are Wes and Coreen supposed to meet you here?" They'd obviously ditched her as soon as they'd gotten to school, and she had stood here waiting for me to come along. Underneath her cool, new front, she was as unwilling as I was to make an entrance by herself.

She really looked terrific, even though I wouldn't have been caught dead admitting that to her after the way she'd mocked me. Didi's beige slacks were tight, just tight enough to look good, but so tight I didn't think I could have worn them without looking around to see if anyone was staring at me. She also had on a champagne-colored cotton blouse so sheer she'd had to wear a lacy camisole underneath. In her high-heeled sandals, she towered over me in my mocs.

She had shortened her hair sometime during the summer, and her springy blond curls hugged her face. But the biggest change was in the new way she carried herself. And her eyes boldly met the glance of every boy who passed. I could tell by the way the boys' eyes just skimmed over me then focused on her that they thought she looked terrific.

Walking along next to her, I didn't feel ordinary any more—I felt downright plain.

"You know, you're really too pretty to let yourself go, Laurie," Didi commented seriously as we walked through the wide double doors into the building. Her voice was soft and unnaturally even, as if she were trying hard not to offend me. "Maybe you should start by pepping up your wardrobe."

She was making me feel worse and worse. Did I really look so awful? I'd be ruined for sure!

"How, Didi?" I asked through clenched teeth, hating the sound of my voice cracking and the way my eyes felt hot and teary. "By buying an outfit like yours? For one thing, I'd look ridiculous. And for another, I'd feel naked. Let's face it, some of us just aren't the sexpot type." I said this with fake lightness, wishing she'd just shut up for ten seconds.

But either Didi didn't hear the pleading tone beneath my sarcasm—or she was enjoying making me squirm. I couldn't tell which. But she didn't stop.

"Don't be silly, Laurie," she insisted. "You could look terrific if you tried. I mean, you look okay now, but it's dumb to be so pretty and not make the most of it. Like your hair—why do you just let it hang there? And your cheekbones! You've got the kind of high cheekbones even models would kill for, but you don't *do* anything with them. You don't even take the time to put your blusher on right." She looked at me hard, as if I were some weird bug she was peering at under a microscope. "It's just smeared all over your face—it makes you look like you've got a cold."

I wished I'd had a cold so I wouldn't have had to put up with her. Even my hateful glare wouldn't stop her. "I mean, it's almost as if you *try* to make yourself look dowdy, Laurie."

"Excuse me for living! Not everyone has to look so dressed up and made up all the time. There are more important things, you know," I said defensively.

"Okay, be like that if you want. But don't come crying to me if you sit at home every Saturday night writing soppy poems while other girls have dates."

That one really hit home. "What makes you think *you're* going to be having so many dates?" I asked her.

"Because I've made up my mind to," she answered matter-of-factly, not at all put off by my question. She stopped and looked at me, her face serious and longing, more like the Didi I used to know.

"Look, Laurie," she said bluntly, "I want to enjoy high school. I want to have fun. And that means dates and parties and boyfriends, not just classes and studying, and poetry. And that means making the right first impression." She reached out a long, mauve-painted fingernail and tapped it against the notebooks. "Keep carrying those around for a few weeks and then ask me why people think you're the intellectual type."

Luckily for me, the homeroom bell shut her up at last. As we rushed forward, I saw that the corridors were almost empty, that most of the kids were already in their homerooms. "Great!

Now we're going to be late. I hope you're happy," I hissed.

But Didi didn't even bat a green-shadowed eye. "No sweat," she said lazily. "Everyone expects you to be late the first day."

Panicked, I opened my notebook to check my homeroom assignment. Didi casually pulled a piece of paper out of her shoulder bag, looked at it, and said, "I'm on the first floor." I was on the second.

Both of us had been to the high school for plays and class fairs and stuff, but neither of us knew the school well. Yet Didi glanced around and confidently started heading in the opposite direction. "See you at lunch," she called. Then she started walking really quickly, and I knew she didn't feel as sure of herself as she was acting.

"Sure," I muttered, heading toward the stairs. "Room 210, Mr. DeVito," I whispered over and over so I wouldn't forget. I took the stairs two at a time. I was furious at myself for wasting time listening to Didi—especially when I didn't want to hear what she was saying about me.

As I ran up the stairs, I noticed that Seven Oaks didn't seem all that different from Wesley. There were the same pukey green walls, the same shiny brown linoleum tiles on the floor, the same babble of voices coming from the classrooms, and the same gray metal lockers lining the corridors. But this was different. This was high school, and the girls I had seen outside were wearing high heels and tight jeans and makeup that made them look grown-up.

If Didi was right, I was already well on my way to being known as an intellectual, serious weirdo.

I made a real effort to push my hair out of my eyes and try to look cool. Then, taking a deep breath, I hurried down the corridor until I found the number 210 in brass above an open, scarred oak door. I slipped into an empty seat in the front of the room just as the final bell started to ring.

I was so flustered at almost being late that it took me a couple of minutes to catch my breath. I felt the blood pounding in my temples as Mr. DeVito called the roll and started to hand out locker assignments. It wasn't until nearly the end of homeroom that I even took a look around the room to see whom I knew. There were a couple of kids from Wesley I knew well enough to say hi to, but no one whom I considered a friend. My mother would have said to look on that as a challenge to make new friends, but it always seemed easy for her to say things like that. You'd have thought that by now she'd know me well enough to realize I wasn't big on challenges. But adults all acted as if being teen-agers had been easy for them. I could never figure out if my mother just didn't remember feeling shy and strange when she was a kid or if she'd been someone for whom everything came easily.

The whole morning passed that way. I'd walk slowly from one class to another, hoping to see kids I knew, brightening up and being overly friendly and gushing when I did, then worrying afterward that I'd seemed too eager.

I was also busy noticing the other girls. Didi was right, I thought as I passed one girl after another in brightly colored jeans or skirts slit up the side or poplin jumpsuits. In my stupid outfit I looked like a grade schooler. Maybe people wouldn't judge Janie Elkins on how she dressed, but I hadn't been born with a brother who was there to guarantee my popularity.

Just as I was moping along, half wanting to go home before the day could get any worse, *it* happened.

Forgetting where my fourth period history class was, I flipped open my notebook so I could read my schedule while I hurried along. I was also balancing my other books and trying to brush my hair out of my eyes at the same time. Maybe if I'd had three hands I could have done it. But since I didn't, there was no way I could have seen the guy coming toward me as I rounded the corner heading to the stairs. Before I knew what was happening, I charged into him. My books fell to the floor.

"Hey, watch it!" I was in such a rotten mood by then that the words came out automatically, even though the collision was my fault.

"Watch what? The ground? Like you?"

I looked up into the most adorable face I'd ever seen, with the bluest eyes in the world. The boy looked down at me in amusement. "You're not going to live to be a junior if you don't start looking where you're going." He chuckled, bending down to pick up my books.

I recognized the long, curly, golden hair. He was the boy in the white Chevy who had scared me to death on my way to the bus stop.

"Sorry," I mumbled, sure he must think I was a total idiot. "You're right. It was my fault." I held out my hand for my book, but he made no move to hand it to me. He just leaned against the wall, casually hooking one thumb in the pocket of his suede vest. With his other hand he flipped open one of my books and read my name out loud. "Laurie Look-At-The-Ground Adams, is that what they call you?"

My face was burning, and I would have been thankful if the tiles on the floor had suddenly parted and swallowed me up—anything to get away from being laughed at twice in one day by this boy. I reached out again and snatched the book from his hand. "I'll try to stay out of your way from now on," I said, trying to act calm.

He just stayed there, grinning in a way that showed off the most darling chipped front tooth. He didn't even seem to mind the way I was practically biting his head off.

His attitude made me feel dumber than if he'd started screaming at me. Feeling trapped with his eyes on me like that, I turned on my heel and walked away, holding my head high, hoping I wouldn't trip.

"Who wants you to stay out of my way?" he called after me, his voice light and teasing, almost a western drawl. "Any time you feel like getting swept off your feet again, just ask for Skip Reardon!"

Once I'd rounded the corner and was on the stairs, I raced down them with legs that felt like they were filled with putty. As I walked down the corridor, my legs felt as if they might buckle under me any second and send me pitching forward flat on my face.

In history class I found myself sitting next to someone I knew—Anna Certowski, a quiet, plain girl with a long, narrow face. Fifteen minutes before, nothing would have made me happier than having someone I knew well in one of my classes. But that didn't seem very important now. The only thing that seemed important was that a guy named Skip Reardon had flirted with me. He'd even acted as if there were something cute and irresistible about a girl wandering around with her shoulders hunched and her eyes to the ground!

Mrs. Porter, the gray-haired history teacher, talked for almost the entire period, but I don't think I heard more than one or two snatches of what she was saying. By the time the bell rang, I had covered three pages of my notebook with doodles centered on Skip Reardon's name.

"Do you have fifth period lunch, Laurie?" Anna asked, sidling up to me in that hangdog way I remembered from last year.

I looked up in surprise, slamming my notebook closed before she could see what was scrawled all over it. I'd forgotten all about her. She was wearing a sacklike knit dress in a sick shade of green. It looked like a dress that might have belonged to her mother. I had always liked Anna, but I knew Didi thought of her as a "grade-A grind." I wasn't exactly excited about walking into the lunchroom with her.

"Oh, yeah. I was just going now," I admitted, knowing I was stuck.

"Wanna walk down together?" she asked. She looked away from me and stared at the blank blackboard. I knew she was afraid I'd say no.

Why did she have to be like such a whipped dog? I thought angrily as I gathered up my books. But when I saw her grateful smile at my "Oh, yeah," it made me feel guilty. What right did I have to put down Anna? I should be nicer to her, I told myself as we left the room. After all, I didn't act any more self-confident around people like Janie than someone like Anna did around me.

"Who do you have for English this year?" I asked, knowing it was Anna's favorite subject just as it was mine.

"Miss Hendricks, third period. How about you?"

"Mrs. Allison, last period. Have you heard anything about her?"

She shook her head. "I don't know much about any of the teachers here, but Miss Hendricks seems all right. Are you still writing poems, Laurie?" she asked, hesitating as if she thought she might be getting too personal.

"I wrote some over the summer, but mostly I swam at the pool and read a lot of mysteries. I wish they'd teach Agatha Christie in high school," I confessed. "I'd rather read mysteries than *A Tale of Two Cities* any day."

One of Anna's rare giggles bubbled out, and

she looked almost pretty. "Maybe the teachers are afraid we'd start thinking of ways to poison them if they encouraged us to read that kind of stuff."

We'd reached the big doors that led into the cafeteria. "From what I've heard," I said as we swung through them, "they ought to worry about kids poisoning the teachers with the food they serve here. It's supposed to be even worse than at Wesley. Ugh!"

I looked around the big, white-tiled cafeteria, searching for Didi. I wanted to ask her about Skip Reardon right away—I was sure she would know who he was. But she was nowhere in sight, and as Anna and I joined the long line at the food counter, my heart sank. If Didi didn't show up, I'd have to sit with Anna or risk eating alone. There was no one else I could spot at the long Formica tables whom I knew well enough to plop down next to. I saw Janie Elkins at a table against the far wall, but she was in the middle of about eight other girls, and from where I was, I couldn't recognize any of them.

C'mon Didi, I prayed as I picked up the chipped white plates that were handed to me. *Don't let me down now.*

But she did. I reached the cashier and handed in my lunch ticket to be punched. Didi wasn't in sight, and I knew I'd gladly sit with Anna rather than take a chance of eating alone.

Then, just as I was carrying my tray to a table, following Anna, Didi walked in. "Hey, Didi, over here!"

"Hi, Laurie!" She waved and started walking

over to where we'd stopped. I hoped Anna didn't notice the look Didi gave her or the unspoken message on her face when she turned to me. It was a message that said, "What are you doing with *her?*"

"I'm glad you're here," I told her when she reached us. "I've got to talk to you!"

She started to say something, but stopped and gave Anna a sneaky, sidelong look. Then in the most phony voice I'd ever heard, she said, "Oh, Laurie, I'm really sorry! I promised these two girls in my homeroom I'd have lunch with them. You don't know them—they went to Plainview last year. But we're together in last period, right? We'll talk after school."

I opened my mouth, then closed it with a snap. Didi was rolling her eyes toward Anna in a hideously obvious way, her way of telling me she wouldn't be caught dead sitting with her. I wanted to throw my tray on the floor and leave. Now I'd be stuck sitting with Anna by myself. I didn't want to be with her, either, but there was no way I'd ditch her in the middle of the cafeteria. I knew all too well how I'd feel if someone did that to me.

"I can't hang around after school," I told Didi, clenching my teeth and giving her a look that should have knocked her dead on the spot. "I'm busy."

"Oh, too bad," Didi said in a way that made it clear she couldn't care less. "Oh, there's Terri and Deborah now! See ya, Laurie. Hi, Anna." She left us standing there. I watched in agony as she went over to two girls with long, streaky blond hair. They both were wearing jeans and blazers, and they had the unmistakable look of Plainview about them. Plainview was the classy side of town.

After that, I couldn't even tell if the grayish roast beef or the puddle of instant mashed potatoes were as awful as they looked. I couldn't even concentrate on what Anna was saying. All I could do was push my food around on my plate and wish I were friends with those sophisticated-looking girls, wish I were talking and laughing with them about boys and music and makeup instead of sitting here with Anna.

I was glad when the bell rang and I could dump off my tray at the pickup window and get away from Anna. Maybe Didi wasn't the only one who was changing, I thought as I headed to sixth period. Last year I wouldn't have been so upset about being stuck with Anna. Had I changed that much over the summer—or had I just changed since Skip Reardon had run me down in the hallway?

I didn't know. But I did know that Didi, as unkind as she had been, had spoken the truth this morning. I decided I was going to learn everything I could about being prettier. And I was going to make sure no one ever called me a bookworm or thought I should be hanging out with squares like Anna Certowski. Even more, I decided not to tell Didi anything about Skip Reardon until I figured out how to get him to ask me out. By the time I was done, she'd never act superior to me again.

Chapter Four

"Laurie!" Mom called from downstairs. "We're ready to leave." We were going to Aunt Mary and Uncle Don's place for dinner.

"I'll be right down," I answered. "I'm just washing my face."

That part was a lie. What I was really doing was trying to finish a poem I'd been working on for the past hour. I finally got the last line right—or good enough for the time being, at least. Then I hid it at the very back of my desk drawer.

Usually I wanted *everyone* to see and admire my poetry. But this was different. This was a poem about Skip Reardon, and I'd have died before I would let anyone know how my crush had blossomed in the space of a few hours. To tell the truth, the poem sort of embarrassed me—I mean, it was on the soppy side.

I wonder what he's like,
The boy who looks so neat.
I only know he makes
My heart skip a beat.

I wonder what he saw
When he looked into my eyes.

Did he see how much I liked him?
Did he notice my surprise?

If he'd ask me for a date,
I know I'd really flip.
I'd give almost anything
To be loved by Skip.

Robert Frost must be turning over in his grave, I thought as I hurried down the stairs, feeling disgusted and pleased with myself at the same time. I was disgusted because I knew it was a dumb poem, but I was pleased because it was the first love poem I'd ever written.

My mother was waiting at the bottom of the stairs. I set down my purse and the paper sack I was carrying and reached for my windbreaker.

"What's in the bag?" Mom asked.

"What, this?" I snatched it up, but it was too late since she'd already seen it. "The electric rollers Aunt Mary gave me for my birthday. I—I thought I'd ask her for some tips on how to use them," I said, making my voice as casual as possible. I didn't want Mom to know how desperate I was to look good. I was afraid she might guess there was a boy involved and start asking me questions about him.

She didn't comment about the rollers, though. She just raised her perfectly plucked eyebrows a little—enough to remind me that mine always looked like a cabbage patch no matter what I did with the tweezers—then turned toward the living room and called, "Jim, we're ready!"

"Hope Mary made meat loaf for dinner," Dad said as he reached in the closet for his corduroy jacket. He bent to kiss Mom's cheek as he slipped it on. "Not that My wife isn't the best cook in the world—but *nobody* can beat my kid sister's meat loaf!"

"Aunt Mary's meat loaf, mmnnn! I hope she made one, too!"

Mom sighed and threw up her hands, but I could see her eyes crinkling with laughter. "I guess I'm going to have to go over that recipe with her one more time. I must be doing *something* wrong."

"Don't worry, honey." My dad patted her arm as we left the house. "Mary can't touch you when it comes to a rib roast."

Mom giggled, and I could tell by the way she raised her hand to smooth back her hair that she was happy. Frankly, I'd never noticed any difference between my aunt's roast beef and my mother's, but I wasn't about to open my mouth.

I guess you could say I couldn't imagine anyone being able to do anything better than Mary. She was a lot younger than my dad, and with her curly auburn hair and freckles, she looked more like she could be my cousin than my aunt. If she were my age, I'd want her as my best friend. Didi was a poor substitute, I thought meanly as I slipped into the back seat of the car. But even as I thought it, I knew it wasn't fair. After all, Mary was ten years older than Didi and me, and she'd worked hard to be as together as she was, going through college on a scholarship, working in the research department at a hospital, and finally settling down with Uncle Don, who was a doctor.

No matter how her life had changed though, Mary had always stayed the same to me. Instead of looking down on teenagers like most adults, she always acted as if I were her equal. She hadn't even let the fact that she was expecting her first baby in just a few more months interfere with our relationship. With all she had to do, she still had time for me.

My Aunt Mary and Uncle Don lived in a white stucco house with a shiny red tile roof on the outskirts of the old area of Plainview. Mary had spent her spare time redecorating it so beautifully it looked as if it should be in *Better Homes and Gardens.*

She hurried to the door as soon as we knocked. She still looked like a school kid in her jeans and sneakers, even though her belly swelled out underneath a T-shirt that had an arrow and the word baby pointing to the bulge.

"You'll never guess what I made for dinner!" She grinned as she kissed each of us separately and hung our coats in the hall closet.

"Meat loaf!" the three of us exclaimed together, laughing along with her.

"How'd you ever guess?" a husky, gentle voice asked. I turned around to see my Uncle Don, who'd walked in from the den on the other side of the hallway. He was as tall and skinny as any boy on a basketball team. He wasn't really handsome, but there was something special about his looks, something warm and friendly and open that won you over before you noticed that his nose was a little too pointy or his front teeth were a little too big or that his hair was a little too stringy.

He looked at my aunt with so much love and pride in his chocolate brown eyes that my heart did flip-flops. Would anyone ever look at me that way? For a minute I imagined how I'd feel if Don was Skip and was glowing with adoration as his eyes met mine. The thought made me feel lightheaded in a way that no poem or novel could have done.

"What's in the bag, Laurie?" Mary asked, and for a second I just stared at her. I was so lost in my daydream that I had forgotten I was in my aunt's front hallway.

"Oh, I brought the rollers you gave me. I thought maybe you could show me how to use them."

Mary didn't raise her eyebrows the way my mother had. To her, my request was perfectly normal. "Sure, honey, after dinner. In the meantime, come see the amazing things we've done to the nursery. I found the most perfect washable wallpaper up in Santa Barbara when we drove over to see Don's folks last weekend. This is one baby who's going to be living in luxury!"

She led us down the hallway to the bedrooms, her step bright and springy even as she asked Mom, "Are these backaches going to last until the baby comes, Lois?"

"Mine did," Mom told her, quickly putting her arm around my shoulders as if she were worried about how I might take what she had said. "But it's different for everyone, they say."

Mary groaned. "Thank goodness I have only another month of work to go. I almost hate to take a leave of absence, but it's reached the point where I'm looking forward to being a lady of leisure for a few months."

"You won't have much leisure after the baby arrives," Mom warned her. Then we both oohed in pleasure as Mary flicked on the light switch.

"You know, if I ever decide to have our place redone, I'm going to force you to help me," Mom said. "You've really got a knack, Mary."

Instead of shrugging or pretending she hadn't heard, the way I usually did when someone complimented me, Mary smiled happily and said thank you. Maybe it was easy for someone who was always being praised, I thought as we walked toward the dining room. I vowed that the next time anyone said anything nice about me, I'd look them straight in the eyes and say thanks instead of hanging my head down and acting as if I'd been insulted.

I'd made up my mind to change all right—and I was going to do it. But maybe I got a little carried away, because one time during dinner, Mary caught me studying the way she was holding her knife and fork and gave me a funny smile. Feeling like a Peeping Tom, I started bolting down my meat loaf and mashed potatoes and kept my eyes glued to my plate for the rest of dinner.

Afterward, my aunt gave me a quick lesson in using the hot rollers and even gave me a package of her own lanolin-treated end papers. "Always use them, Laurie. They'll keep the ends of your hair from splitting and drying out."

Thank goodness she didn't question me about my new-found interest in my looks. I didn't feel like telling even her about my run-in with Skip. Instead, we talked about my new teachers and the classes I'd be taking and about Mary's search for a mother's helper and her plan to go back to work at the hospital after the baby was born. I had trouble keeping my mind on what she was saying. I kept thinking about Skip Reardon and mentally reviewing every item in my closet, trying to figure out what to wear to school the next day.

"Well, you must be tired after the big day," Mary said as we went back to rejoin the others in the living room.

"Mmmm." I faked a yawn, going along with the excuse so she wouldn't guess that my thoughts were somewhere else. "I'm just about ready to crawl into bed."

Luckily, both my mom and dad had been busy all day, so we didn't stay much longer. But when we got home, I didn't go right to sleep. Instead, I curled up in bed with a plate of chocolate chip cookies and a glass of milk and stared in the direction of my open closet door, looking at the clothes hanging there. I finally decided on my navy slacks, blue-and-white-checked shirt, and high-heeled sandals. It wasn't the best or the slinkiest outfit I owned, but I didn't want the change in me to be too sudden or too noticeable. I set the alarm for six thirty, so I'd have time to do my hair.

It was only as I was drifting off to sleep that I realized my books were still neatly stacked on the desk where I'd dropped them after school. For the first time that I could remember, I'd forgotten all about doing my homework. I gritted my teeth, then reached out and reset the alarm for six o'clock. I wondered how Didi's new girlfriends managed to look so good and do their homework, too.

Chapter Five

"Your hair looks lovely, dear," Mom said the next morning as she set a plate of eggs—scrambled soft the way I liked them—and toasted raisin bread in front of me. "What do you think of Laurie's hair, Jim?"

Dad half-raised his eyes from the newspaper. "Nice," he murmured before going back to the sports page.

"But," Mom added, and I held my breath, knowing what was going to come next, "isn't that a little too much makeup for tenth grade?"

"Oh, Mom, all the girls are wearing eye shadow and mascara this year!" I wailed.

She narrowed her eyes in the direction of

mine, then bit her lip. I guess she knew it was useless to argue. But when she came back in from the kitchen and sat down, I compromised. With a finger, I wiped away some of the blue smudge-crayon I had put on my eyes. I could always touch it up when I got to school.

"Much better, honey," she said. "And I really do like your hair. Did it take long?"

"Oh, no," I fibbed. "It only took a couple of minutes."

Actually it had taken me so long to get all the rollers in right that I'd only been able to skim my reading assignments. Everyone knew the teachers never expected kids to work the first week of classes, anyway.

At least, that's what I told myself as I left the house and headed for the bus stop. I also told myself that I didn't care if Didi was waiting for me or not, even though I had a hard time convincing myself of that. Didi and I had been best friends for so long that I couldn't imagine being in high school without hanging out with her. The idea that she might prefer her new friends to me gave me a heavy feeling in the pit of my stomach.

When I spotted her sitting on her front steps, however, I walked faster, feeling as if an enormous weight was lifting off my shoulders.

"Hi, Laurie!" She jumped up and hurried down the walk—that is, she hurried as much as she could in her high-heeled red leather mules and tight black chino jeans. With her pale curls pulled back with red plastic combs and her bright red leotard, she looked just like a photograph I'd seen in the papers of a dancer from the Los Angeles ballet company. She moved just as gracefully, making me feel clunky.

"Hey, new hairdo!" she exclaimed. "A definite improvement."

"Glad you approve," I said with a trace of sarcasm. "I'd hate to have to go home and redo it." But I was secretly thrilled that she thought it looked good. At least I was making progress.

She was peering at me critically out of the corners of her eyes as we walked. "And you've done your makeup! Now you're getting the idea, Laurie. You already look ten times better than you did yesterday."

"Do you really think so?" I asked, not even caring if she could hear the anxiety in my voice now. I *did* want to be pretty, and the new, sleek Didi seemed to know all the tricks.

"Well, you're no Bo Derek," she kidded, "but you'll do."

I noticed that Janie Elkins wasn't at the bus stop and guessed it was her turn to get a ride to school. Today, there was a calmer atmosphere as everyone waited for the bus. First day jitters were over.

"You're going to lunch with us today, aren't you?" Didi asked when we sat down on the bus.

"Who's us?" I asked, already knowing but wanting to hear.

"Me and Terri and Deborah, of course. Or do you feel honor bound to hang out in the cafeteria with Anna?" she asked snidely.

"Don't be so snobby about Anna! She's okay."

"You *want* to eat lunch with her every day?" Didi had a smug smile on her face that made me want to sock her, but how could I hit her just for knowing how I felt?

I shrugged. "Sure, I'll eat with you guys. How come Deborah and Terri aren't on the bus?"

"They ride in with a bunch of junior girls from their neighborhood. Hey, you should see this guy who's in my history class! Gorgeous! His name's Barry Knox, and somebody told me he just moved here from Chicago. Have you seen him?"

"Not that I know of. What's he look like?"

"Oh, I don't know, just gorgeous. Of course, he's only a sophomore. But I think it's all right to go out with a sophomore if he's something special, don't you?"

"I guess so. Why wouldn't it be?" I was puzzled.

"Oh, you know. Terri was saying yesterday that she wants to date only older men—preferably seniors—though juniors would be considered." Didi giggled, and by her next remark I could see that underneath her new clothes and makeup, she was the same Didi as always. "I mean, I'd be scared to death to go out with a senior, wouldn't you?"

I mumbled in agreement. As I gathered my books to my chest and climbed off the bus, I wondered what Didi would say if she knew I was scared of going out with anyone—and even more scared that no one would ask me. She seemed so confident, and I couldn't imagine her feeling the same way.

The morning went by quickly as I was busy

daydreaming in class about Skip Reardon and keeping an eye peeled for him in the corridors. By the time I headed for history class, down the same hallway where I'd collided with him the day before, I felt jumpy as an exposed nerve. But that tall, perfect body was nowhere in sight. I had a bleak, letdown feeling as I slipped into my seat in the classroom. I barely murmured to Anna when she said hello.

Now I have that problem to deal with, I thought miserably, almost sure Anna would be waiting for me after class to go to lunch. I hated to be mean to her, since I knew all too well how awful it was to be left out of things. But I also wanted—with a desperateness that I didn't quite understand—to be part of Terri and Deborah's clique. I didn't doubt for a second that if I dragged Anna along to lunch Didi would never speak to me again.

All the time Mrs. Porter was talking, I was busy thinking up excuses. I couldn't tell Anna I was sick, since she'd see me at lunch and know that that wasn't true. I couldn't tell her I had to talk to Didi in private, since she'd obviously see we weren't alone. I almost hated Anna for existing. If she didn't, I wouldn't have this awful problem to deal with!

Luckily Anna solved it all for me, and I didn't have to show her what a cowardly, fair-weather friend I was. As soon as class was over, she stood up and said shyly, "Maryann Abbott has lunch this period, too. Do you want to eat with us, Laurie?"

I was thankful that Anna was so shy she

never looked anyone in the eye when she talked. I'd have died if she had seen the look of relief on my face. "Thanks, Anna, but I told Didi I'd eat with her and some other kids today. See ya, okay?"

I just rushed the words out, then practically ran from the room, not especially proud of myself but not willing to show up at the cafeteria with Anna, either. And Maryann Abbott! She was definitely a flake. Boy, next to her, Anna was a star!

When I saw Didi standing in the food line by herself, I felt better than I had all day. I wondered if Didi's new pals had dropped her already. I hoped they hadn't because I wanted to get to know them, too. But in a way it would have served her right for the snotty way she'd treated me yesterday.

Didi looked really happy to see me. "Here, Laurie," she called loudly when I was still a good ten feet away. I realized with a start that she was as ill at ease standing in line all by herself as I would have been.

I slowed my step to a saunter to torture her, but she didn't seem to notice. "I've been saving you a place," she announced loudly for the benefit of the kids behind her who were already glaring at me for cutting in. In a softer voice she added, "Terri and Deborah said they had to run up to their lockers. They'll be a little late."

"Oh?" I studied the menu board on the wall so she wouldn't see that I was really more interested than I sounded. "Ugh! Macaroni and cheese!

Don't they know that a lump of macaroni with yucky orange cheese on top is not a meal?"

"You think that's bad? Look at the vegetables. Buttered beets or stewed tomatoes," Didi moaned. "If macaroni's not a meal, then beets and stewed tomatoes aren't vegetables."

We didn't stop complaining until we were at the table, but that didn't stop us from loading up our trays. "I'm eating this only so I can get to the Boston cream pie," Didi insisted, shoveling in her macaroni like a starving castaway. I could tell she was as hungry as I was, but it was against the rules of the student body not to complain about the food. "Oh, look, here come Terri and Deborah."

They were walking toward us, their trays perfectly balanced, and I loathed them for their poise. Both of them had on blue blazers, though the one who turned out to be Terri was wearing a red plaid skirt while Deborah's was camel's hair. They looked more like stewardesses carrying meals to passengers than high school sophomores about to dig into cafeteria food.

They were okay, though. They spent the first half of lunch talking mainly to Didi. While yesterday I might have tried to stay unnoticed, I forced the new me to talk a lot. I wanted these girls to like me, and I was sure they wouldn't if I didn't act as if I could keep up with them. By the second half of the lunch period, they were both starting to include me in the conversation. Terri even turned to me and said, "I like your shirt, Laurie."

When she said that, I was all ready to pretend I hadn't heard. But then I remembered the promise I'd made to myself yesterday. I looked her right in her round blue eyes and smiled. "Thanks, Terri. To tell the truth I'd do anything for a blazer like yours."

"You like this old thing?" she asked, her voice rising in surprise as if I'd said I liked to eat roasted toads. "I've had it for ages."

I was just about to tell her I'd be glad to take any hand-me-downs she might have when the bell started clanging.

"Yuck! Biology lab next!" Deborah said, widening her eyes in horror in a way that looked so good I knew I'd practice it when I got home. "How can they expect us to slice up amoebas after eating this gruesome food?"

"You can't slice up amoebas, dummy," Terri corrected her. "They've only got one cell, remember? Or maybe you don't expect to pass biology."

"One cell's too much for me!" she joked. "Especially on a full stomach."

I was just gathering up my tray, thinking how much I longed for the day when I'd be able to talk comfortably with Terri and Deborah, when Terri suddenly let out a little squeal.

"Oooh, look who just walked in! Darn it, why couldn't they have given me lunch just one hour later?"

"Who now?" Deborah drawled, looking around the lunchroom. She made a funny face, crossing her eyes at me and Didi. "I mean, the girl's got so many crushes you'd need a computer to keep

track of them. The cast of her dreams reads like
the roster of the Seven Oaks Senior High football team."

Terri gave a little snort of impatience. "There's
only one man in my life, stupid. The rest are all
boys. Look, he's getting in line."

Deborah shook her head, then made a little
circle around her temple with her forefinger.
"The girl hasn't been the same since she met
Skip Reardon at the pool this summer, poor
thing."

Automatically my eyes darted toward the cafeteria line. There he was, Skip Reardon, *my*
Skip Reardon, looking even cuter than yesterday.
He was wearing baggy olive drab pants and a
khaki shirt. If he looked a little bit like he was
in the army, all I can say is that I was ready to
enlist.

I didn't even realize I was staring at him until
he tilted his head and returned my stare. He
gave me a playful wink and a smile.

"See! He's winking at me!" Terri was so excited
that the plates on her tray were rattling against
each other.

"I don't know how to tell you this, kid,"
Deborah said, her voice all gruff and mock serious, "but it was pretty plain to see that he
winked at Laurie."

They were all watching me then, and I could
spy a new respect edging into the look Didi was
giving me.

"You know *him*?" she asked, in a voice that
was little more than an awed whisper.

"Oh, no," I sputtered. "I mean, not really.

Hardly at all." I don't know why I got so nervous. It wasn't as if everyone in the lunchroom was able to read my mind or see into my dreams and know that I was already hopelessly in love with Skip Reardon. Still, I could feel the heat burning in my face, and I knew I was blushing furiously.

"I'd better run," I said quickly. "I'm going to be late for class."

But before I could make my getaway, Skip Reardon sauntered toward us. He walked with long, easy steps, and I was sure by the little half-smile on his lips that he knew every girl in the room was watching him. Who wouldn't stare? After all, he looked more like a rock star than a mere high-school kid.

I felt as if his deep blue eyes were burning right into me. I forgot about Terri and Deborah and even Didi. All I was aware of was Skip Reardon and that smile on his face. If another boy had looked at me that way, I'd have been furious or thought he was too conceited to live. But with Skip, all I felt was a shiver of excitement. Was he going to talk to me? Or was he coming over to say something to Terri, whose face had gone blank the instant he left the cafeteria line?

I couldn't stand there another second—I'd be so humiliated when he ignored me. I clutched my books even tighter to my chest and headed away from Skip and the girls, trying not to run toward the door.

Behind me I heard his voice, musical and a

little mocking, calling, "Hey, Laurie, you running away from me again?"

It took all my courage to turn around, but I knew Didi would never let me live it down if she thought I was running away from a boy. I forced myself to turn and smile at him. "I'm just late for class, as usual!" I called back, amazed at how casual my voice sounded. Nobody would guess I was a trembling wreck inside.

This time I couldn't doubt that his smile was just for me, and I couldn't keep myself from smiling back. The last thing that caught my eye as I hurried from the room with the next-to-last bell clanging in my ears was the sight of Terri, Didi, and Deborah, all staring after me. They were round-eyed with surprise. I realized as I half-walked, half-ran up the stairs there was something else in their faces—envy! Those girls were actually jealous of *me!*

Chapter Six

That night I stood in front of my mirror, experimenting with new hair styles and makeup. Maybe Skip really *was* interested in me, and if there was even the slightest chance of that, I wasn't going to blow it by showing up at school looking anything less than glamorous. I tried to study, but my mind was filled with the image of a tall, handsome boy with silky curls and eyes the color of the sky. I forced myself to read twenty pages on the life of the cell, but biology left me cold. Before I even knew what I was doing, I was sitting at my desk writing another love poem. How could a poor, humble cell hope to compete with a handsome guy for my affections? My new poem was called "Just One Boy." Before I had it at the back of my desk drawer with the other poem about Skip, I covered the margins of the page with doodles of hearts and arrows and our initials intertwined all over the place. This is what I wrote:

> *What would I do if a genie appeared,*
> *To make all my wishes come true?*
> *I wouldn't ask for gold or diamonds galore,*
> *Or trips to a South Sea shore.*
> *All I'd request is just one boy,*
> *And that one boy is you.*
>
> *If I had three wishes,*
> *I wouldn't need two.*
> *Who needs wishes to spare?*
> *A date with the guy with the golden hair,*
> *Is the only thing I'd ask.*
> *And that one boy is you.*

The next morning I was out of bed at six-thirty so I could wash and dry my hair before setting it on the hot rollers. I was starting to see that looking good could be a full-time job!

At lunch, Terri, Deborah, and Didi kept asking me all about Skip, and I kept insisting I didn't really know him. "Honest!" I said in exasperation when Didi prodded me for the umpteenth time, asking how long I'd known him. "We bumped into each other in the hall one day, and that's all."

Didi glared at me, refusing to believe I wasn't keeping something from her. But to my surprise, Deborah jumped to my defense.

"That's right, Laurie, keep it to yourself. Believe me, if Skip Reardon was drooling all over me in the lunchroom, I wouldn't be letting anyone pry the truth from me."

"What's the big deal about Skip Reardon, anyway?" I asked, as if I couldn't be less interested in him. "I don't even know who he is."

"He's just the best-looking and most talented boy in the junior class," Terri insisted. "Boy, I'd give anything to be you! I mean, he's almost a rock star."

"You mean he looks like a rock star," I said.

She shook her head emphatically. "No, he *is* a rock star. He's got his own band, the Bonkers, and he even played a gig in Los Angeles this summer!"

I'd never even heard anyone use the word gig, and at first I couldn't even figure out what Terri was talking about. I just looked at her blankly, and she started talking real slow and carefully, as if I were mentally defective.

"He's had a band since junior high," she explained in a hushed voice. "Skip plays electric guitar, but the other guys in the band don't go to Seven Oaks. I think they all live a little farther down the coast. And," she added, giving me a satisfied look that showed how special she felt for knowing all this, "he writes a lot of his own songs."

"That's right," Deborah chimed in. "Carolyn Huntzberger went out with him a few times last year, and she says he's just waiting until he graduates next year so he can go to L.A. and break into show business."

We were all quiet then. I guessed the other girls were as impressed at the idea of someone breaking into show business as I was. I felt depressed. There was no way a guy like Skip, who was already busy planning his future in the world of rock 'n' roll, would be interested in a girl who wrote silly poems.

Janie Elkins picked that minute to walk up to the table. To my surprise, Terri and Deborah greeted her brightly. "Set down your tray and join us," Deborah suggested, sliding over on the bench to give Janie room. I wondered if they were only interested in her because she had a popular brother who was a senior. Then I immediately felt guilty. After all, neither of them had been anything but friendly to me, and I had no superstar relatives at Seven Oaks.

"We've been talking about the *fabulous* Skip Reardon," Didi said in a way that implied she thought he was anything but (but which I was sure was just resentment at feeling left out). "Everybody seems to know who he is but me."

"Skip Reardon?" Janie frowned. "I don't really

know him, but I think he's the one Bob's always calling the school goof-off."

"He's a friend of your brother's?" Terri's blue eyes were shining.

"Well, not exactly. Skip's on the football team—if he stays, that is. According to Bob, the coach told him to start cracking the books and forget about music and girls if he wants to stay on the team. He sounds like a real runaround to me."

"What do you mean?" I asked.

Janie giggled. "His nickname this summer was One-Date Reardon. Bob says he has a new girl waiting for him every day after practice."

"Oooh, why can't I be one of them?" Terri moaned.

"Don't be stupid!" Deborah snapped. "Who'd want a date with someone they'd see only once?"

Me, I said to myself. *Me*.

But I didn't want anyone else to know how I felt, so instead of saying one more word about Skip, I turned to Janie. "Gee, I really like your blouse. Where'd you get it?" I asked lightly, determined to change the subject.

I didn't see much of Skip for the next couple of days. Only a glimpse of his shiny curls at the other end of the hallway, the sight of his back on the stairs. Once I saw him when I was rushing to get to class on time, after having wasted precious minutes fixing my makeup in the girls' room. He was running, too, so we didn't even say hi, but for days afterward, I lived on the memory of the wink he gave me.

I was obsessed, and I knew it. Would he like this dress? Did he have a weakness for pale turquoise eye shadow? Which of the girls I passed in the halls or sat near in class had been lucky enough to date him? Would my turn ever come? And if it did, would I make a fool of myself, or would I die of heartbreak if he ignored me afterward?

One day early in October I was on the way to school, about a block from Didi's house, when I heard the whoosh of car tires behind me. Skip's car zoomed to a stop at the curb.

"Well, I can't believe it! Laurie Adams—and actually watching where she's going for a change!"

My heart was in my mouth. Automatically I smiled back at him. I opened my mouth to say hello, but my throat was so dry and tight I couldn't say anything. So I just smiled all the more, terrified that I looked like an idiot.

"Why don't you hop in, and I'll give you a ride—save you from getting run down in the crosswalks?" he asked lightly. I couldn't help but wonder how many times he'd given girls rides to school.

"Oh, I can't," I told him, and the real regret in my voice embarrassed me so much I could feel my face growing warm in the early autumn chill. "I always stop by Didi's to take the bus with her on the way to school," I added, making my words as casual as I could and praying I sounded as if guys offered me rides every day of the week.

His eyes stared, as if he thought I was crazy

for saying no. Or maybe he was just surprised.
I felt so uncomfortable that I was about to start
explaining how much I'd really rather go with
him if I could when he suddenly said, "Well,
that's okay. I like a girl who's a loyal friend.
How about a Coke after school? We could go to
the Hut."

"Oh—uh—sure," I stuttered. "That would be
nice."

Before I even got the chance to hate myself
for acting like I was accepting an invitation to
tea, he was slowly pulling away. "I'll meet you
by the parking lot door after classes. See ya,
Laurie."

I managed to paste a weak smile on my lips
as he drove away, and it was only willpower that
kept me going, moving one foot ahead of the
other automatically. I felt dizzy and weird—and
absolutely wonderful.

Strangely, I didn't tell Didi anything about
my date with Skip. Since the Hut was at the
other end of town and only kids with cars hung
out there, I knew there was a good chance she'd
never find out I had gone there with him. As
excited as I was about his asking me to go with
him, I was afraid to have anyone else know. If
this was going to be my one date with One-Date
Reardon, I'd rather not be laughed at by my
friends when they learned about it.

I guess nobody noticed that I was acting
strange—or maybe I was a better actress than I
suspected—because nobody commented on my
being extra quiet or walking around with my
head in the clouds. But that's how I felt all day.

I looked at the clock about once every ten minutes, impatient for the time to pass until I'd see Skip again. I couldn't stop thinking about how happy I was because I knew that if I did, I'd be scared. Scared he wouldn't like me, scared I wouldn't know what to do, scared his friends would think I was a bore. But even the terror was exciting.

I was so nervous that by the time I was waiting for Skip to show up at the parking lot door, I felt ready to call the whole thing off. I had rushed out of English class to the closest bathroom mirror. I'd carefully brushed my wavy hair and pulled one side back with a tortoise-shell barrette, retouched the lavender shadow on my eyelids, added more charcoal crayon liner, and fixed my fading blusher.

I rushed so much that I was early, and I had to do my best to look casual as other kids passed me by on their way to their cars. I shifted from foot to foot, brushed imaginary lint off my slacks and sweater, stared blankly at my opened geometry book, took as many deep breaths as I could, and ordered my palms to stop sweating. If this was what dating was like, maybe I'd be better off remaining a wallflower for the rest of my life, I thought glumly.

Then I saw him walking toward me—and suddenly every second of agony seemed worth it. My heart started pounding rapidly. He was busy talking to another guy, so he didn't notice me at first. I had plenty of time to study him. He *was* perfect, from the casual toss of his golden hair to the loose, catlike way he walked. I felt awkward and ungainly, like a little kid caught peeking in on the grown-ups' party.

I didn't want to be caught staring at Skip, that was for sure, so, as they came closer, I switched my attention to the other guy. He was pretty cute, too, though nothing like Skip. He reminded me a little of my Uncle Don, actually. He was tall and wiry but with bigger shoulders than Skip's. His straight brown hair was medium long, and he had the kind of face you would have called nice instead of handsome. But next to Skip he was dull. Dressed in a letter sweater and gray slacks, he looked preppy, while Skip, in his faded jeans, boots, and suede vest, looked super-hip.

The other boy must have felt my eyes on him, for he gave me a shy but warm smile that set the butterflies in my stomach to rest. Then he said something to Skip that made him look my way. Skip winked and waved. They stood talking, about fifteen feet from me, while I held my breath and tried to look as if I was used to leaning against doorways waiting for boys to take me to the Hut. Then Skip laughed and said loudly, "Okay, Jeff, see you later." After giving me a little smile, the guy started walking back the way they'd come.

"Boy, am I glad to get out of this place!" Skip exclaimed as he took me by the elbow and started steering me toward his car, jangling his keys in the other hand. "Another year at Seven Oaks should push me right over the edge."

I giggled, more to cover up my nervousness than because he'd said anything funny. "I don't know. . . . I sort of like it."

He raised his eyebrows in amazement. "Yeah? Then sometime you should try to explain to someone like Jeff Aldridge why music means more than football."

He got in on his side of the car and opened the door for me from the inside. I slid in. "Is Jeff the guy you were talking to? He doesn't look like a jock. But why do you play football, anyway, if it bores you?" I knew I was babbling, but I'd have done anything to cover up how excited I was at being alone in a car with a boy for the first time in my life.

"Nah, Jeff's no jock," he explained, gunning the motor so I had to strain to hear him. "He's just one of those guys who thinks it's a breeze to get good grades and who can't see that some-body might not care about getting into college more than anything else in the world. He's tutoring me so I can stay on the team."

"Why don't you just quit?" I asked curiously as he pulled out of the parking lot and started heading in the direction of the Hut.

"It's my old man," he admitted. "My dad would kill me if I got bounced off the team. He thinks being a singer and having a band is ridiculous, and if he gets his way, I'll be in school another four years. Right now I can't tell him I have no intention of going to college."

I nodded, as if I had this kind of conversation every day.

"So I keep the old man happy by staying on

the team and not flunking out. But it's not my style, you know?" He laughed. "I mean, can you imagine anyone who's got all their marbles liking school and rushing home to crack the books? Crazy, huh?"

"Mmm," I murmured, hunching down in the seat and staring out the window. Just a few weeks ago, I'd been one of those "crazy" people—and I knew that if Skip had even guessed it, I wouldn't be here right now. I guess that's why I added, "I couldn't care less if I never had to read another book as long as I lived."

And you know what? I didn't even feel a tiny twinge of guilt when I heard that lie in my own voice.

Chapter Seven

The Hut was about a ten-minute drive from school. I was glad Skip kept the radio turned up so loud to the local rock station that it was almost impossible for us to talk. He sang along to the music while I did my best to relax the muscles of my neck and shoulders so I didn't look as if I were waiting to be taken to the electric chair. I was too antsy to start thinking of things to talk about once we were out of the car, so I thought about what the Hut would be like instead.

Even back in junior high, I'd heard about the
Hut. It was the "in" place where Seven Oaks'
most popular juniors and seniors hung out.
You didn't *have* to be popular to sit around in a
booth there, but in some kind of unspoken
agreement, the kids who were out of it didn't
bother to show up. I'd spent all summer worrying
that I wouldn't even know whether I was supposed to show up or not by the time I was a
junior, and now here I was, only a sophomore
and headed right that way. And with a guy who
was obviously part of the right crowd!

Skip parked at the curb just a few doors
down from the Hut's plain red brick exterior
and hopped out of the car. I didn't want him to
think I was prissy or unliberated, so I opened
my door myself and stood on the curb waiting.

He didn't put his arm around me or anything
like that as we went inside. Still, I didn't doubt
that everybody could tell we were together, which
made me feel happy and confused at the same
time. Happy, because I was with him; confused,
because I was afraid all the kids were whispering, "There's Skip's latest one-date chick."

If I hadn't known that the Hut was *the* place
to go, I would have been disappointed. It didn't
really look much different from Cookie's Coffee
Shop, where I'd gone sometimes after school
the year before. It had the same cracked ma-
roon plastic on the booths, the identical scarred
gray linoleum tables, the same long counter,
and a jukebox that looked pretty much like the
one at Cookie's. The only difference was that

the walls here were covered with framed photos of Seven Oaks sports teams and graduation classes.

A few people motioned to Skip to join them, but he just shook his head, leading me to a booth near the back. "This way they've got to come to *us* if they want to talk," he told me, his eyes crinkling up when he smiled and his voice low as if we were sharing a little secret.

"Are you sure you wouldn't rather sit with your friends, Skip?" I asked quietly, worried that he was just being polite. I wondered if he would much rather be with the pretty little brunette in the cheerleader's uniform who had waved frantically when we'd walked in, then frowned when she'd noticed me. Or if he'd rather be with the four girls who sat sitting and giggling at one of the front tables and who'd chimed "Hi, Skip" together as we passed.

"I know *them* already," he said matter-of-factly. "Now I want to get to know you."

Thank goodness the waitress came up then! I mean, no guy had ever said anything like that to me before. I wished I had something smart to say or that I knew how to flirt or act coy. Instead, I just acted like he hadn't said anything. "I'll have a Coke and an order of french fries," I mumbled—to the waitress, not to him.

"That's all, Laurie?" he asked. When I nodded, he shrugged. "Well, I'm starving. I'll have the usual, Dolly," he told the middle-aged, plump woman who was standing there with her order pad out.

"Dolly? Is that her name—or do you call everyone that?" I blurted before I knew what I was saying.

But it was okay. He laughed as if I'd told some hysterical joke. "No, I don't call everyone that. Dolly's her name."

"You must come here a lot if she knows what you're going to order. What's the usual?"

"Cheeseburger, fries, and a vanilla shake. Yeah, I guess I do hang out here a lot. I like to stop in after practice or at night after rehearsing with my band."

"Tell me about your band," I said quickly, remembering some article I'd read once that said you should always try to get a date to talk about himself.

It turned out I'd said the best thing possible. Skip's face lit up and he started rattling on a mile a minute, telling me all about the Bonkers and where they'd played. There were so many places it was easy for me to look impressed, even though I'd never heard of most of them. Here I'd been living other people's lives through reading books while Skip had been really living, playing gigs and driving down to L.A. to catch new acts at the clubs there. I was sure he must think I was from Mars or something, but he didn't seem to notice. He was too busy telling me about the new amplifier he wanted to buy. It was all beyond me. He could have been speaking about space modules for all I knew. But I didn't care. I was too happy just watching the flash of his beautiful teeth when he smiled and gazing into those deep blue eyes, memorizing every line and expression and freckle on his face.

The waitress brought the food, and I decided the french fries were at least a thousand times better than the ones at Cookie's. I didn't say so, though—I knew it would sound stupid.

I was so hypnotized by him that I didn't even notice how steadily the room had been filling up. "Another Coke?" Skip asked when we'd eaten, and I just nodded dumbly, straining my brain in an attempt to come up with another subject to talk about.

"What do you need, Skip?" a friendly voice asked. I looked up to see the guy Skip had been talking to earlier standing by the booth, only now he had a waiter's jacket on.

"Hey, Jeff, you taking over for Dolly already? We'll have another Coke and a vanilla shake."

I thought it was kind of rude of Skip not to introduce me to Jeff. Even if he was the book-ish type, he *was* helping Skip stay on the football team and seemed friendly enough. For a moment, while Jeff went to fix our drinks at the fountain, I wondered if maybe Skip was ashamed of being with *me*, but I quickly put that out of my mind. After all, if he hadn't wanted to be seen with me, he'd never have brought me to the Hut in the first place.

I decided that Skip just must have forgotten his manners. I didn't want to make him feel tacky, though, so when Jeff came back with our order, I just smiled brightly and said, "I guess Skip thinks we know each other already. I'm Laurie Adams."

"Hi, Laurie," he said, giving me a big grin. "I'm Jeff Aldridge."

"Yeah, Jeff Aldridge, the one-man dynamo," Skip hooted. "The only guy in the world who can play football, get straight A's, and work after school." He shook his head in pretended despair, rolling his eyes at me in helplessness until I had to giggle. "Now why can't I be like that?"

"Hey, man, don't forget that I can't play guitar," Jeff said good-naturedly. I thought it was nice of him not to take offense at Skip's teasing.

"He seems nice," I said after Jeff had gone to wait on someone else.

"Oh, Aldridge is all right," Skip said, even though he didn't sound enthusiastic. "He's just not my idea of a fun guy, you know? I mean, why be young and alive if you're not having fun, right?"

"I'll drink to that," I kidded, raising my glass. Right that instant, Skip's philosophy made plenty of sense to me. After all, hadn't I spent the first month of the semester more interested in clothes and makeup and gossip than studying? This was the new me, and I was enjoying it.

But funny thing is, it was the side of me I'd been trying to hide that got Skip's attention and interest. He was telling me about a song he'd been slaving over that still didn't sound right. "Sometimes I just get stuck for the best rhyme," he said, "and then, no matter how many times I go over it, I just can't get it to work."

"What's the line you don't like?" I asked.

"Well, the drag is that it's at the very beginning of the song. Here's how it goes: 'When you're not with me, it's just not right. I go to bed sleepless every night. But when you're beside me, I'm a different man....' Then it's got the same rhythm more or less. 'Da da da da da da dum, da da da dum.'"

It came to me so fast that the words were rolling off my tongue before he'd even finished tapping out the beat on the table top. "How about this?" I asked. "'If you can't make me happy, then nobody can'?"

"Hey!" His palm smacked the table so hard that the glasses moved. "That's great, Laurie! You didn't tell me you write songs."

"Oh, I don't really. I mean, I used to write a lot of poetry—when I was a kid. Now I've been working on some lyrics." I thought that sounded pretty good.

I guess Skip did, too. He was already scrawling the new words I'd given him in his notebook. "You know, we oughta work on some things together. What do you think? I've really dried up lately as far as lyrics are concerned—I'm much more into writing the tunes, anyway. Maybe what I need is a collaborator. What do you say? Want to try your hand at a song or two? We could be the new Sonny and Cher."

"Sure," I agreed, hardly daring to breathe, not able to believe my ears. Then I started laughing. "But don't compare us to Sonny and Cher!"

He looked blank. "How come?"

"Well, look what happened to them."

"Not us, Laurie." He put his hand over mine, and I forgot all about the Hut. It was as if we were the only people in the world. "We're going to stay together."

Those were the words that kept going through my thoughts long after Skip had dropped me off at the library. He hadn't kissed me good-bye—just reached up and sort of ruffled my hair—but I don't think any kiss could have meant as much as those words did. *We're going to stay together.* Could it be? Did Skip Reardon really want to be *my* boyfriend?

It was Mom's volunteer day at the hospital, so the house was quiet when I got there. That was a relief. I could hardly wait for my parents to meet Skip, but I didn't want that to happen until I knew he wasn't going to drop me the way Janie said he'd dropped everyone else. I figured I'd find out soon enough since he'd said something about getting together next week after football practice to work on a song together.

I dashed upstairs and kicked off my shoes, throwing myself on my bed with a notebook and pencil so I could dash off a song before Mom came home and it was time for me to help her fix supper. But I was too excited to be able to think of anything. In just one day my entire life had changed.

Pins and needles is the only expression that describes the way I felt. I tried to read my English assignment but stopped after mindlessly going over the same paragraph four times. I flicked through the clothes in my closet. I rearranged my shoes. I stood by the window gazing outside and wondered how I ever could have thought that twilight was the loneliest time of the day. Today twilight didn't seem sad at all. This is it, I thought. This is what it's like to be in love.

Finally, I sat down and wrote a song. It was a song he'd never see, a secret song I'd written just for him and me. I called it "My Reflection," and it went like this:

I looked in the mirror
And what did I see?
I saw a special person,
And that new girl is me.

I'm not really different,
But I'm not the same.
I've got the same face;
I've got the same name.

My cheeks gleam with color,
My hair falls in curls.
But that's not what sets me
Apart from other girls.

It's a certain boy
Who's made a new me.
And if he likes this Laurie,
I'm happy as can be.

Tomorrow, I promised as I heard my mother's key in the door, I'd start working on a song to show Skip, one that wouldn't let him guess how I felt.

Mom must have noticed my glaze of happiness and thought it was something else because after I finished setting the table, she looked at me strangely and asked, "Is anything wrong, Laurie?"

"Wrong?" I shook my head, knowing if I told her I'd just fallen in love, she'd say something about how it was only a crush. "No, I'm fine. I just had a lot of work in school today. I'm tired, I guess."

"You don't want to catch cold so soon in the semester, dear. Try going to bed earlier. After all, you wouldn't want to miss the Glee Club tryouts. They'll be coming up soon, won't they?"

"Glee Club?" I'd forgotten all about that. "Yes, I guess they're soon."

"You don't sound very interested, Laurie," Mom said, her voice turning stern. "You are planning to try out, aren't you?"

"Sure, I guess so. I don't see why not."

I tried weakly to put some enthusiasm in my voice. How could I be expected to get all turned on by the idea of Glee Club when I'd soon be writing songs with Skip Reardon? I must have sounded bored to her, though, because after dinner I overheard Mom say to Dad, "I don't know what's wrong with that girl lately. She's in another world."

"Just a phase," Dad said, and I could picture

him patting Mom's hand across the table. "She's growing up, dear, and this is an important time for her."

I *am* growing up, I thought as I scraped the dishes and rinsed them before setting them in the dishwasher. This *is* an important time for me. But it's not a phase. Love was much more than a phase—it was forever. For the fiftieth or so time since the afternoon, I whispered aloud the words Skip had spoken: "We're going to stay together." I couldn't imagine being this happy all the time, but I was more than willing to give it a try!

Chapter Eight

The next day, I went from the heights of happiness to what was pretty close to the depths of despair.

From the beginning of the day, things went wrong. When I stepped out the front door, I noticed that the weather had changed. It was only October, but the wind rippled my hair and numbed my nose as if it were December. The sky looked gray and heavy, as if it might snow, though that was close to impossible in this part of California. As it was, it was so damp I was sure it was going to rain. I just hoped I didn't get drenched before the bus came! I dreaded to think of what a good storm could do to my freshly made waves.

The closer I got to Didi's house, the more thankful I was that I'd worn my new beige corduroy coat, even though I'd worn it only because nobody had seen it yet and not because I'd realized I was going to need it. But as I hurried down the street, I cursed myself for not having worn a scarf or a hat.

That's how the day started. And it got worse. By the time the bus pulled into the parking lot, it was drizzling just enough to make a mess of my hair. By the time I got to the girls' room to comb it, it was half straight and half curly. The only way I could keep from looking terrible was to wet it all down. To make matters worse, my eye makeup had run. Before I had the chance to touch it up, the first homeroom bell rang. I stormed to my locker, glaring at Didi as I left her humming cheerily to herself in front of the sinks. Her hair curled naturally, so she looked just fine.

Then my geometry teacher hit us with a pop quiz—and I'd done no more than skim the chapters it covered! Thank goodness it was mainly a recap of stuff I remembered from ninth grade. Still, I had a sinking feeling that I'd get by with only a C. My eyes swam with tears of anger and defeat.

Everyone was in a rotten mood at lunch. It seemed to have been the day for quick quizzes. Didi had been given a surprise essay test on a history lesson she hadn't read, and Deborah was feverishly trying to read her biology notes at the cafeteria table. Janie rushed by, explaining she was just going to grab a sandwich and study in the library. I guess it was just my own guilty conscience, but I thought she was implying that we were too shallow for her to bother with.

Outside, the raindrops, fatter and more serious now, splattered against the big windows. The storm dimmed the room, causing the fluorescent lights to cast a yellow glow that made everybody look sickly.

The food itself was a greasy, lumpy beef stew that looked as if it might have been made two or three months before. But it wasn't the food that made my stomach do somersaults. That happened when Terri joined us, her lips set in a thin line, a high flush dotting her cheeks under her makeup.

"Well, I'm never talking to Julie Parr again, and you can quote me on that!" she said in a high voice as she slammed down her tray and sat next to Deborah. "To think I considered her my friend!" She sniffled, and I wondered if she was going to cry. But she didn't. She just added in a little, hurt voice, "And when I remember how upset I was that she wasn't going to be having lunch this period. Boy, am I dumb!"

"What's wrong?" Didi asked, as curious as she was concerned.

We were all waiting for an answer, and I guess Terri liked being in the limelight because her face suddenly brightened. "Oh, she's just a little shrew," she said, not sounding so mad now. "She knows I have a crush on Skip Reardon, so what does she do? She gloats over the fact that she is meeting him for lunch today. Can you imagine? I don't care who he has lunch with, and it would be fine with me if he was madly in love with Julie, but I don't think someone who's your friend should be so smug!" She sighed, then lifted and lowered her shoulders as if she were dismissing Julie Parr with the movement.

I couldn't move. I just sat there, my fork clutched in my hand, feeling as if all the grayness outside were coming in to swallow me up. With a start, I realized Terri was talking to me.

"Look, Laurie, I don't know what's going on with you and Skip, but don't pay any attention to Julie. Or to me," she added sympathetically. "I know he doesn't know I'm alive. I'm just mad at Julie. Besides, I'm sure he's having lunch with her just so she'll help him with his math homework. She's a whiz at numbers even if she is only a sophomore. But"—she gave Deborah a meaningful glance—"I certainly don't expect her to be invited to anyone's house after school if I'm going to be there."

Deborah tossed back her blond hair and smiled calmly. "I seem to remember trying to tell a certain someone that Julie Parr was a little snip *ages* ago," she said, the look on her face announcing that Terri could expect no sympathy from her. "Well, I've got to run. If I don't get to class early and study in peace, I'll be in tenth grade for the rest of my life." She walked away.

I realized I wasn't the only one in a lousy

mood. But surely nobody else could feel as miserable as I did.

Or could they? Just then Didi's face turned a sickly white as she stared across the cafeteria. "Now, what's wrong with *you*?" I snapped, no concern left for anyone but me.

"It's Barry Knox," she whispered.

"Who?" Terri seemed back to her usual good humor. I wished I could say the same.

"Barry Knox," Didi groaned. "The gorgeous guy from my history class. He's got his arm around that girl!"

We all watched the black-haired boy walk to the door with his arm draped casually across the shoulders of a tiny redhead. "Win a few, lose a few," Terri said resignedly. "Looks like we're the old maids' table."

That did it. I grabbed my tray and jumped up. "I guess I'd better run, too," I said, my lips so stiff I wondered how I was getting the words out. "I've got to fix my face before class," I explained, even though I'd just freshened up before lunch. All I wanted to do was get out of there before Skip walked in with Julie Parr—or before I humiliated myself by bursting into tears in front of everyone.

One-Date Reardon, I said to myself as I rushed blindly through the halls, my head down so no one could see the tears welling in my eyes. And I'd already had my one date!

I ducked into a booth in the nearest girls' room and slumped against the wall, biting my lip so I wouldn't cry and dabbing at the tears that had already started trickling down my face.

I was acting like a fool, and I knew it. After all, I told myself, who was Skip Reardon to me? Just some guy who'd bought me a Coke.

But even after I'd calmed down and splashed some water on my face, I knew Skip meant much more than that to me already. I'd felt that we were so *right* together the day before in the Hut. I'd even gone to sleep dreaming of the two of us writing songs together, maybe even becoming a famous songwriting team!

Worst of all, ever since I'd heard from Janie that Skip wasn't in the habit of seeing any girl more than once, I'd spent all my energy convincing myself that it would be different for me.

Slowly, anger won over my hysteria. I was mad at Skip for his leading me on. He'd probably thought the line I'd suggested for his song was dumb. He probably told all the girls he went out with to write songs with them. I decided that I'd show Skip Reardon that not every girl at Seven Oaks High could be had at the snap of his fingers.

I was mad at myself, too, for getting carried away by the first boy who'd paid me any attention. Now I looked on my quiet behavior at the Hut as pathetic. He and Julie Parr were probably laughing right this instant at the way I'd hung on his every word! How in the world could I have thought that a guy like Skip, who could go out with any girl in school if he wanted, would be interested in ordinary me?

The rest of the day passed in a gray funk that matched the weather outside. I moped through the halls and didn't pay any attention to anything a single teacher said, slouching down at my desk so I wouldn't be called on. The only time I perked up was when the bell rang for the last time, and I did that for two reasons: one, because I was relieved to go home without a glimpse of you know who, and, two, because there was no way I'd let Didi guess I was upset about anything.

On the bus, I talked nonstop about the bad weather and schoolwork, hardly giving Didi a chance to say a word. I didn't want her to mention the conversation at lunchtime. I guess I went overboard, because just before the bus reached her stop, she turned to me and said, her voice rising in surprise, "Well, Laurie, I guess we were all wrong about your secret romance with Skip, huh?"

"What do you mean?" I was so startled I practically screeched the words.

"Nothing," she answered, shaking her head. "It's just that I figured if there was really something going on between you two, you'd be totally crazed about his having lunch with some other girl. But it doesn't seem to bother you at all."

I looked at her out of the corner of my eye, trying to figure whether she was being mean and just putting me on. But she was casually buttoning up her trench coat and gathering her stuff together, and I knew that if she'd been baiting me, she would have been watching for my reaction. So it was easy for me to say offhandedly, "Really, Didi! I told you we hardly even knew each other. It's not my fault if you wanted to blow it all out of proportion." Then, remembering her own letdown in the cafeteria, I added, "Sorry about Barry Knox and that girl. I know you were hoping he'd ask you out."

"Oh, you never know. He still might." She stood up as the bus came to a stop, a brave smile on her face, and I knew she was enjoying her tragic moment. "Anyhow, there're other fish in the sea. Why don't we go to the Hut later in the week and see if we can catch any?"

"The Hut! But that's just for juniors and seniors," I said as we got off the bus.

"So?" She shrugged. "Everyone'll respect us for daring to crash."

Before I could say another word, she lifted her hand in half a goodbye wave and walked off. I spent the next couple of blocks to my house trying to figure out how I could get Didi to forget about going to the Hut without letting her know I'd already been there and without her guessing how much I dreaded running into Skip with his latest girl.

By the time I reached my house, I felt low and alone. "I think I *am* catching a cold, after all," I told my mother as soon as I'd hung up my coat and dragged myself into the kitchen. She was stirring up sauce and layering noodles for lasagna. It was one of my favorite meals, but now just looking at the pot bubbling on the stove made me feel sick. "I think I'll go upstairs and take a nap."

She wiped her hand and pressed the back of it against my forehead. "You don't feel feverish, but you look awfully pale," she said. Even though

I felt bad for making her worry, I wasn't about to admit it was only my heart that was broken.

"Oh, I'm sure it's nothing," I insisted weakly. "I just need to lie down."

But she was already at the refrigerator, pouring me a glass of orange juice and shaking some vitamin C's out of the bottle. "Here," she ordered, handing them to me, "take these and tuck yourself in bed. I'll wake you for dinner."

"I don't think I want dinner," I told her, feeling like crying again.

She shook her head, smiling slightly. "Maybe your appetite will come back by six-thirty. If not, I'll make you a bowl of soup, okay?"

As I walked heavily up the stairs, feeling as if I was weighed down with three hundred pounds of lead, I had a sneaky suspicion my mother realized my problem didn't have anything to do with the flu. But even though I wished I could tell her everything, I knew I wouldn't. There were some things I couldn't expect her to understand. She was so on top of things I couldn't imagine any boy having jilted her when she was my age.

By the time I reached my room, I felt so listless it was all I could do to take my shoes off before lying down on the bed. I'd planned to lie there and cry, but now that I was there, I discovered I really was tired. Before I knew it, I was asleep.

A knock at the door woke me. "Laurie, it's dinner-time!" Mom called lightly. "Feel up to eating?"

To my surprise, I did. I almost told her I'd

have just a bowl of soup—since that seemed more in keeping with my visions of how to act when you'd been hurt by a man—but hunger won out over heartbreak. "I—I'll try to eat some lasagna," I answered. "I'll be right down."

Why should I punish myself? I thought as I put on my shoes. To tell the truth, I was finding moping too draining for me. I knew also that if I wasn't acting normal by tomorrow, all the girls at the lunch table would notice. So, with a firmness that surprised me, I put the whole ugly incident out of my mind and went downstairs to dinner. I'd prove to myself that no dumb boy had that much power over me.

I kept to my vow after dinner, too, going straight to my room after washing up so I could catch up on my schoolwork. For the first time since school had started, I went to bed with all my assignments for the next day finished. I wish I could say it gave me as much of a sense of satisfaction as Skip's asking me out had. But it didn't. I still felt sad and abandoned.

Chapter Nine

From the time I woke up the next morning, I made a strong effort to push Skip Reardon out of my thoughts. I just about succeeded.

The rain and overcast skies of the day before had vanished, and the day was bright and clear. I felt strong and powerful. Not even the falling maple leaves that flitted onto the sidewalk in front of me as I walked to Didi's could change my mood. I wasn't like the maple leaf, drooping and dying in the autumn. I was like the palms that grew right beside them in this part of California, thriving all year long, no matter what came to pass.

I managed to keep my spirits up all that day and the next, even though I didn't see Skip and, for all I knew, never would again. My willpower kept me going. Each time I could prove that I wasn't letting him get me down, I felt better about myself.

Jeff Aldridge's big smile and friendly greeting two days later helped. "Hi, Laurie!" he called as we passed in the hall. "How come you haven't been coming by the Hut lately?"

Before I could do anything but wave and yell hello, he was gone, swept away in the tide of students heading in the other direction. But I felt good that he'd remembered me and seemed to accept me with or without Skip. I decided then that I'd go to the Hut with Didi the next afternoon, Friday.

She was dumbfounded. "You'll really do it?" she asked in amazement when we were heading home on the bus. "I thought you said only juniors and seniors hang out there."

"You're the one who said we were going to be brave and crash, right? Don't tell me you're chickening out now?"

"Of course not," she said angrily, and I knew she'd been thinking of it. "But, Laurie, what if no one talks to us?"

"There's always Coreen and Wes," I said sarcastically.

"That's not fair," Didi grumbled, still upset that Coreen had decided it was dumb for her to hang out with her kid sister.

"I'm sorry," I said, and then couldn't help but add, "I know a boy who works there."

She didn't say anything else, but I was sure she was dying to ask me how I knew a boy from the Hut and who he was. Maybe it was mean of me to act so conceited, but I couldn't help getting back at Didi for the snotty way she'd treated me just a few weeks before.

The next day I took extra-special pains getting ready for school, knowing I was going to be on display afterward. I wore my best jumpsuit, a dark brown one that had a small gold pattern in it. It brought out the highlights in my hair and the gold glints in my brown eyes. I spent twice as much time on my hair as usual, pulling the waves off my face with shiny combs. I strained my eyes blending green and beige shadow on my eyelids. By the time I was through, I figured I could pass for a junior any day—even if I still wasn't a glamour girl.

Maybe because we were both nervous, Didi and I didn't discuss our after-school plans. It was as if we had an unspoken agreement not to include Terri, Deborah, or anyone else. This was our little scheme, and we'd fail or succeed on our own.

Didi had taken special care getting ready today, too. Her hair was so bright and shiny she must have washed and rinsed it three or four times. It was fluffed loosely around her face. She was wearing the same outfit she'd worn the first day of school—her best slacks and sexy camisole top. I could tell by the way her hand kept flicking to her hair to pat it into place that she was nervous about going to the Hut. For some reason, her edginess made me feel calmer. The only thing I really worried about was that somebody would see us arriving by public bus instead of in a car. I figured we'd get off at the bus stop after the Hut and walk back so no one would see how we got there.

It wasn't until after lunch that I started worrying about running into Skip there. What would I do if he strolled in with some new girl on his arm? The prospect made me so nervous that I spent most of my time in class mentally practicing imaginary conversations. "Hey, Skip, how're you doing?" "How's the music business?" "Haven't seen you around, Reardon." Everything I came up with sounded phony and not like me at all. I decided just to smile.

Strange as it seems I was walking down the hall practicing my smile for the imaginary Skip when I found myself actually smiling at the real him! The expression froze on my face as if I'd been stopped in a game of statues.

"Laurie!" he said, grinning in a way that made me melt inside and forget I was supposed to be mad at him. "I've been looking for you all week." Before I had a chance to look as if I couldn't care less, he'd grabbed me by the elbow and steered me away from the traffic in the hall.

"I could have kicked myself for not getting your phone number," he went on—or at least those were the words I heard over the loud thumping of my heart. "And there're so many Adamses listed in the phone book I couldn't figure out which one was yours. Hey, you still want to get together and try our hand at a song, don't you?"

He'd tried to call! He'd actually sat down and gone through the phone book trying to figure out which Adams was me! For the first time in a week I felt really happy. It was as if all the misery I'd felt had been just a dream.

"Sure I do, Skip." I couldn't believe my voice sounded normal or that I hadn't gone into a dead faint.

"Well, why don't we get together over the weekend?" he asked. "I always go out with the guys after the game, and there's more practice tomorrow afternoon, but we could hang out tomorrow night or Sunday. Or how about after school today?"

"I can't today," I told him. "I promised my friend Didi I'd go to the Hut with her."

A shadow passed over his face. I couldn't figure out why, but he didn't seem thrilled about my plans. "You been going there a lot?"

I laughed, carefree and happy now that I knew he was still interested in me. "How could I be going there a lot, silly?" I asked. "I was just there for the first time this week with you—

that doesn't give me much time to become a regular."

"Yeah, that's true, I guess." His face relaxed again. "Why don't you wait for me there, and I'll give you a ride home? I've got to meet with Aldridge right after school, but I'll be by afterward."

"Okay," I agreed. "That'll be great. If you can drop Didi off at her house, too, that is," I added.

"No sweat. How you girls getting there without a car?"

"Oh, her sister's dropping us off," I lied.

For a few moments we just stood there smiling at each other, and I knew with all my heart that Skip was as glad to see me as I was to see him. Talk about feeling on top of the world! If someone had come along and offered me a million dollars right that second, I don't think I would have heard them.

Neither of us could help hearing the bell for class, though, since we were standing right under it. "Better run," Skip yelled over the noise. "I'll see ya at the Hut." His hand lightly touched my shoulder, sending shivers through me. "And this time you're not getting away without giving me your phone number!"

I barely remember the rest of the school day. A cloud of joy carried me to my next class and straight through till the last period. How could I concentrate on anything? All I could think about was the way Skip had smiled at me. And he'd asked me out for Saturday night!

By the time I grabbed my coat from my locker

and went to meet Didi, I'd already made up my mind not to say anything to her about Skip meeting us. I was afraid she'd chicken out and leave me there all alone as I waited for him to show up.

She was waiting for me inside the front doors. "Let's walk to Miller Avenue to get the bus," she suggested offhandedly. "It's such a nice day after that drizzle yesterday, I wouldn't mind walking a few blocks."

"Not to mention that you don't want other kids to see you catching a bus to the Hut."

"Do you?"

"Don't worry." I laughed. "I've already decided we should get off the bus at the stop past the Hut."

That made Didi laugh, too, and we walked up the street, like co-conspirators on a spy mission instead of two teenage girls on their way to a restaurant. Once we'd boarded the public bus, we both became quiet, thinking about the Hut and wondering what was going to happen there.

When I stood to pull the rope to signal our stop, I felt its vibrations go through my body. I was strung just as tightly as that plastic signal cord. In one more hour I'd be seeing Skip!

"You walk in first," Didi hissed when we were almost to the door. I realized with a shock that our relationship had changed since school had started. This time I was the one who was brave and knew what to do. For the first time since we'd met, Didi was voluntarily giving up the lead and practically begging to be the follower.

Maybe I'd have minded going in first if I

hadn't known Skip was going to be showing up. Just knowing he'd be there gave me confidence. Even though it was Didi by my side, I was already thinking of myself as Skip Reardon's date.

I almost lost my nerve, though, when we got inside the door and I saw only strange faces lining the booths and the counter. Fortunately it was still early enough for the place to be only about a third full, so at least we could sit down. I spied the booth where Skip and I had sat last time. It was empty. So, as if I were part of the inner circle of regulars, I led Didi back there and sat down.

Her eyes were round as she took everything in, staring at the pictures on the wall and craning around to see if there were any kids there she knew. I almost called Dolly by name when she came over to take our order, but I didn't want Didi to know that the reason I was unafraid of coming here was because I'd been here before.

"I'll have a Coke and a cheeseburger, please," I said. "Didi?" She was in such a fog I had to give her a little kick under the table.

"Oh! A vanilla Coke and an order of onion rings, please," she said, taking off her jacket.

As soon as Dolly had left to put in our order, Didi leaned back and sighed. "Gee, we're really here! At the Hut!" A frown quickly replaced her blissful look. "But, Laurie, what if nobody talks to us? What if we just sit here like two dress shop dummies?"

"Don't worry, Didi. If that happens, I'm sure

we can live with it. Besides," I added mysteriously, "I don't think it will."

Didi ignored my mysterious hint and started talking. "Oh, guess what? I ran into Barry Knox in the hall today, and he gave me the biggest hello! I think he's going to ask me out soon. What do you think?" But before I got a chance to answer, she was bubbling on. "Maybe he comes in here. Do you think so? He's only a sophomore, but he's from Chicago, so he must be used to going wherever he wants. Boy, would it ever be neat if he walked through the door!"

I didn't understand what being from Chicago had to do with hanging out at the Hut, but I didn't say anything. I didn't think it was exactly cool to sit in the middle of a place talking about how wonderful it was to be there, so I changed the subject fast, talking about the new blouse Deborah had been wearing that day, a blouse I was sure was real silk. Even my mother has only three silk blouses.

Of course, all the while I was talking, I was sneaking little looks at the wall clock behind the soda fountain. After we'd been there for only about forty-five minutes, I asked Didi if she'd order another Coke for me while I dashed to the girls' room. I wanted to look my best when Skip walked in.

But Skip didn't get there first. Didi and I were busy complaining about our history classes, both of us trying to act as if we were terribly interested in our conversation, when I saw Jeff

Aldridge walk in. I almost fell over when I realized he was heading straight toward us!

"Hiya, Laurie," he said, giving me that nice, open smile.

"Hi, Jeff," I answered, so glad he'd bothered to say hello that my smile must have lit up the room. "This is my friend Didi. Didi Callahan, Jeff Aldridge."

Didi smiled bashfully, and I realized that in spite of all her big talk about boys and dating, she was pretty unsure of herself.

"Going to work now?" I asked casually. "Or would you like to sit down?"

He shook his head. "Thanks, but I've got just enough time to change before I relieve Dolly. I just stopped by to let you know Skip said he'd be a little late. He had to stop to pick up some guitar strings out at Music City."

"Oh—well, thanks," I murmured, avoiding the deathly look Didi was shooting me across the table.

"In the meantime, why don't I change, then treat both of you to Cokes?" He grinned. "It's the least a gentleman like myself can do," he kidded.

When he'd gone, Didi leaned across the booth. "Laurie Adams, what's the big deal?" she hissed, but I could tell from her voice she was more excited than mad. "You told me you hardly knew Skip. And who in the world is this Jeff Aldridge?"

"Oh, he's a friend of Skip's," I said breezily. "The only reason I didn't mention that Skip was coming was because I was afraid you'd cop out if you thought I had a date. You should be glad he's meeting us. He knows everybody—you'll get to meet some neat juniors."

"Yes, that's true, I guess," she said—sort of grudgingly, I thought. "But why did you lie to me about Skip? I thought we were best friends," she added, stressing those last words.

"Look, Didi, I'm sorry about that. But I really don't know him very well. I mean, you'd hardly call us an item," I added, not mentioning that I wished we were exactly that. Then bragging got the best of me. "He *did* say something about maybe going out tomorrow night, though."

"Laurie, how fabulous!" she squeaked, shutting up quickly as Jeff walked over and delivered our Cokes.

I'd expected her to be sullen or jealous of Skip's asking me out, but she soon told me the reason why she wasn't. "Gosh, do you think he'd maybe fix me up with one of his friends sometime?" she asked dreamily. "Or even one of the guys in his band?"

"Maybe. But I can't ask him yet. Let's wait and see what happens. After all, they might not call him One-Date Reardon for nothing." It was easy for me to say that now that I was on the way to Date Number Two.

"Well," she said softly, "if it doesn't work out with him, you can always settle for that guy Jeff. He hasn't taken his eyes off you since we walked in."

"Don't be silly," I said, even though I felt a

little pleased. "Jeff's just being nice 'cause he's Skip's friend."

"Oh?" she murmured, and I could almost see the wheels turning in her brain. "Maybe *I'll* do a little flirting with him then."

"Really, Didi, you're terrible!" I'd meant to say it jokingly, but the words came out sounding harsh. Didi looked at me sort of funny. *What's wrong with me?* I wondered. *Do I want every guy in Seven Oaks High School to be interested in only me?*

But before I could dwell on that thought, I saw those adorable blond curls in the doorway. Skip was working his way through the now-crowded aisles to get to our booth.

No, I thought blissfully as he made his way toward us, *I don't want every boy—just one.*

Chapter Ten

I'll never forget that day Didi and I went to the Hut together, because that was the day that I think of as the real start of my relationship with Skip. When he slid into the booth next to me and draped his arm loosely over the back of the seat so it just skimmed my shoulders, I just knew he wasn't One-Date Reardon any more. I still couldn't believe I was the girl he'd decided to concentrate on. But I was.

Oh, he didn't ignore Didi or anything like that. He shared his beautiful smile with both of us and even went out of his way to make small talk with Didi. But it was plain to see that I was the girl he'd come to the Hut to be with.

I was only half listening while he and Didi kept up a steady stream of conversation, although I was careful to smile and look interested any time he glanced my way. No, I was too busy marveling at how matter-of-factly I'd accepted what would have seemed like an out-and-out fantasy only a week before: I was sitting here with a boy I'd have thought was far out of my reach, and already I was beginning to think of myself as his girl.

"Wake up, Laurie Adams!" Skip's husky voice jolted me out of my reverie. "You didn't even hear what I said, did you?"

"Oh—sure I did. You and Didi were talking about last week's assembly."

The smile vanished, and he looked a little hurt. "That was ages ago. As a matter of fact, I was just telling you I've got to rehearse tomorrow night, so we can't work on a song. But why don't you come over, anyway? That way you can get an idea of what the band sounds like. And we can always stop here and grab a bite after the session."

Didi's green eyes flashed at me. It was easy to see she was dying to come along. But I didn't feel it was my place to invite her. "Where's rehearsal?" I asked, knowing my parents would never allow me to go if it was being held someplace unchaperoned.

Skip must have figured out why I was asking. "No place dangerous," he said, chuckling. "In my garage. My folks'll be home, but they don't allow what they insist on calling 'that loud, grating music' in the house. What do you say? I can pick you up and drive you home afterward."

"Sounds fine to me," I told him. "I don't see why my parents wouldn't let me." I hoped that didn't sound babyish to Skip, but it was going to be my first honest-to-goodness date, after all!"

"Then it's a deal!" He tore a sheet of paper from his notebook. "Write down your address and phone number, and I'll give you a ring after practice to let you know when I'll be by."

"Uh-oh, that reminds me! I'd better be getting home right now, or I won't be going any place tomorrow night." I quickly scrawled down the information. Then we all stood up and got ready to go. Didi's tongue was practically hanging out in the hopes of getting an invitation. But Skip didn't say another word about the rehearsal.

"You guys leaving already?" It was Jeff, clearing off the table and sounding like he was really sorry we were going.

"The ladies'll turn into pumpkins if I don't have them home by five o'clock," Skip quipped.

"And you're going home to do your trig assignment, right?" Jeff asked, sounding a little stern.

"Boy, you crack the whip harder than the

coach!" Skip's tone was light, but I thought I could hear a little peevishness creeping in.

If Jeff had heard it, he overlooked it. "Just want to make sure you stay on the team, fella," he said, slapping Skip lightly on the shoulder. "See you at the game. Good to see you, Laurie," he added politely. "And nice to meet you, Didi."

"Thanks for the Cokes, Jeff. See you soon."

As soon as we were outside, Skip turned to me, his face flushed with anger. "Don't tell me Aldridge is buying my girl Cokes!" he said. "What is it with that guy? Isn't it enough he's taken over my studying and my football training without horning in on my dates, too?"

"Oh, it was nothing, Skip," I said, feeling happy at his jealousy. "He was just being nice. I think he felt sorry for us because we had to sit all by ourselves waiting for you," I added lightly, turning it into a joke.

"Sure, sure," he said, opening the car door, his fit of temper already gone. "I'll bet you girls were just pining away without me."

We all laughed at that. As I slipped into the front seat between Didi and Skip, I felt strangely relieved that I was on my way home. Being somebody's girlfriend was new to me. I couldn't have been happier about the whole thing, but at the same time, I welcomed the chance of being plain old me at home with my parents for a while.

"Bye, Skip. Bye, Laurie," Didi said as she jumped out of the car in front of her house. Then she stuck her head back in. "Call me later," she ordered, giving me one of those

I've-got-something-important-to-talk-about looks. I just nodded, since I was sure I already knew what she wanted to talk about. I had no intention of nagging Skip about letting Didi come to his rehearsal. Not just because I didn't dare bug him, but because there were some things I didn't want to share with anybody, not even my best friend.

I hadn't realized how much Didi's being there had given me nerve, though. Without her in the car, I felt tongue-tied and twitchy, and there was a lump in my throat that made it hard to tell Skip how to get to my house. Somehow I managed to give him the directions, then I sat back stiffly against the car seat and wished I knew what to do and how to act. Deborah or Terri wouldn't be struck dumb by a guy's presence, I was sure. They'd be able to talk up a storm. But even when I tried putting myself in their places, I couldn't think of a thing to say. I just sat there in agony, afraid Skip must think I was the most boring girl in the entire school.

So I pretended I was listening closely to the radio and puzzled over how I could be so happy being with Skip and still be so eager to get away from him.

When we got to my street, I pointed. "It's the clapboard house on the left."

He pulled up and cut the engine. "Nice and old-fashioned," he commented. "Like you."

"What do you mean?" I asked, my heart in my throat, positive he was laughing at me.

He didn't say anything for a minute. Then he reached over and took my hand and gave it a squeeze. "I mean down to earth, not stuck-up or spouting about women's lib and college boards like some of those girls at Seven Oaks."

"Oh." I didn't know what to say after that. I didn't want to ask him what was wrong with women's lib or college boards, so I just said in a squeaky voice, "Well, thanks for the ride. And I'll talk to you tomorrow, I guess."

He let go of my hand and started the car, and I thought he seemed just as nervous as I was right then. "Call you in the afternoon," he mumbled, already starting to fiddle with the radio dial as I got out.

"Good luck tonight," I said as I got out. I wished I could see him play, but the game was being played away from home, and I had no way to get to it.

For some reason, it was lots easier for me to feel excited about Skip when he wasn't there. I guess that was because I didn't have to do anything or say anything then. As soon as I was on my way to the front door by myself, I felt lighthearted and bubbly, and I could hardly wait to announce that I had a real date for tomorrow night.

But Mom wasn't there. There was a note on the kitchen blackboard that said, "Visiting at Mrs. Miller's." I knew that with the way old Mrs. Miller liked to talk, Mom wouldn't be home for a while. There was a chicken casserole in the oven and salad greens in the bowl on the sideboard, so all I had to do was set the table. When I was done, I went upstairs to read my history assignment, but the text seemed duller than ever. After I spoke to Didi, who, as expected, put in a pitch to come along with me to Skip's, I took out the poems I'd written about Skip and read them until I heard Mom opening the front door.

I popped downstairs and went into the kitchen, where I was sure I could find her. She was mixing the salad dressing when I swung through the door and leaned against the refrigerator.

"Thanks for setting the table, dear. We'll be eating as soon as your father gets home."

"Need any help?" I asked, even though I could see she didn't. I wanted some excuse to stay there and talk.

"No, not really," she murmured absentmindedly. "Everything's ready. Your father's got to eat and run—he's got a big contract coming up and has to go back to the office tonight for a few hours."

"There's a good movie on TV we can watch together," I suggested as I poked around in the refrigerator looking for some soda.

"No homework?"

"Oh, that's all done," I said breezily. It wasn't, but the TV movie was about a boy who played with a rock band, and I wanted to watch it so I'd have something to talk over with Skip the next night.

"What's up, Laurie?" Mom asked suddenly. "It's not like you to watch my every move."

"Oh! Well, actually, I wanted to ask if it was okay with you if I went out after dinner tomorrow night. I've got a date."

There, I'd said it! Just saying the words made

me feel older and more mature, as if Mom and I were equals now and not mother and daughter. But if I'd expected an earth-shattering reaction from her, I got none. No jumping up and down or clapping her hands. She just kept tossing the salad, taking time out only to smile and murmur, "That's nice, dear. A boy from school?"

"Skip Reardon," I said, announcing his name as if I expected her to know who he was. Then I realized that of course she had no idea that any girl in the tenth or eleventh grade would have given her right arm to be seen with him. "He's very good-looking and talented," I said importantly.

That got her attention. She stopped making the salad dressing. Wiping her hands on her apron, she turned to face me. "And nice, too, I hope?"

"Of course he's nice!" I said, insulted. "Really, Mom, would you expect me to go out with Attila the Hun?"

"Now, Laurie," Mom began in the voice she uses whenever she thinks somebody's getting excited over nothing, "you know I didn't mean it that way. I know you'd only accept invitations from nice boys."

I almost started laughing. Here I was, keyed up to begin with, and my mother was talking as if I spent almost all of my time sifting through hundreds of invitations from guys deciding which one I should honor with my company! But I could see by the thoughtful look on her face that she was starting a serious speech.

"You know, Laurie, we haven't really discussed

dating before," she said tactfully, not mentioning the obvious fact that there'd never been any reason to, "but as long as you'd like to go out tomorrow, we may as well do it now. There are going to have to be certain rules for you to follow."

"I know that, Mom." I sighed. She was certainly doing her best to ruin my happiness by spouting off about rules and regulations before I'd had even a single date!

"Don't roll your eyes, young lady!" she ordered, but her mouth was twitching at the corners, and she didn't sound the least bit put out. "You're better off hearing this from me than having to listen to a long lecture from your father. Don't you agree?"

"Yes, ma'am," I answered quickly, much more willing to listen to her now that I'd heard the alternative. My dad's great and all, but whenever he takes it into his mind to have what he refers to as "a good long talk" about something, he gets very somber and long-winded, repeating everything three times or more to make sure I don't miss the point. It comes from talking to builders all day, I imagine. You know, one brick or window in the wrong place and the whole house is screwed up.

Now I hung on Mom's every word, letting her talk so she could get everything said before Dad got home.

"Your father and I have already discussed this—knowing it would come up someday—and we decided that ten o'clock on school nights, as long as your homework is finished beforehand,

and eleven-thirty on weekends are the right
hours for a girl your age."

"Eleven-thirty!" I protested automatically, not
knowing when other girls my age had to be
home. "But, Mom, all my friends are allowed to
stay out later than that!"

"If you follow the rules and show us you can
act in a responsible manner, dear, we can talk
about a later curfew."

I grumbled a little under my breath but didn't
put up a fight. Whenever my mom starts talking
in that stilted way and uses words like responsible, there's no changing her mind. I'd worry
about talking her into letting me stay out till
midnight some other time.

"Now," she said in a different voice, one that
hinted her serious speech was over, "why don't
you tell me something about this boy Skip and
what your plans are for tomorrow? You're going
to need your father's permission, too, but it
might be better if you told me first." She smiled
for the first time since we'd started talking.
"After all, fathers do tend to be stricter about
what their little girls do."

I couldn't see how Dad could still think of me
as a little girl when I was practically sixteen
years old and taller than my mother, but parents are funny that way. I followed Mom into
the living room, my mind churning as I tried to
think of what to tell her. I wanted to make sure
I told her what she'd like to hear—without
lying, of course. I knew her well enough to be
sure she wouldn't be terribly impressed to learn
he had a band. She'd probably decide that that

meant he was a punk rocker or something and that I should sit home and wait for some boy with what she usually called "a promising future" to ask me out. Being a rock star wasn't my mother's idea of a promising future, but since I didn't know too many future brain surgeons, she'd have to make do with Skip.

"He's on the football team," I said as soon as we were seated side by side on the couch. "And he's interested in music."

Mom's ears perked up at that. "Oh? Did you meet him at the Glee Club tryouts?"

"No, they haven't had those yet," I told her, which was perfectly true.

"He's in one of your classes?"

"No, he's a junior. Everybody in the school knows him, though," I added proudly. "He's real popular. He composes music, and we're going to work on some things together, setting my poetry to music that he's written," I explained, hoping I was making him sound like an artistic classical composer headed straight for the symphony orchestra. That would score points with my mother, who was real big on anything that could be considered culture.

It worked. "How nice," she said, and I could tell she approved. "A musician! And what are you going to do tomorrow night? See a movie?"

"Well, not exactly." I squirmed on the couch, trying to put the words together so they'd sound like the description of what a mother would consider a proper evening out. "We were just going to go to his house and listen to music and maybe write some things together. His parents are going to be home, so it's not as if we'd be alone. There'll probably be some other kids there, too," I said, the words coming out in a rush.

Mom nodded. "That sounds fine to me, Laurie. As long as we get to meet him and you give us the number at his house in case we have to get in touch with you. Will he be able to pick you up and bring you home, or will you need a ride?" she asked—as if *anybody* would go on a date where their parents had to deliver them.

"He has his own car," I told her. I saw her brow wrinkling and added quickly, "Don't worry, he's a good driver."

"Have you driven with him before?"

I didn't want it to sound like I'd been seeing Skip behind her back, but I didn't want to tell a fib, either. "He gave Didi and me a ride home from school today," I explained. "That's when he asked me out."

The sound of Dad's key clicking in the front door lock saved me from having to add anything to my explanation. Mom reached over and ruffled my hair. "I don't think your father will have any objections, honey. And I'm glad you're making new friends at school this year. You can't spend all your time studying, you know."

If Mom knew how little time I'd spent studying lately, she might not be so pleased about my brand-new social life!

Chapter Eleven

When Skip showed up to pick me up the next night, he put on his best manners, and I knew before we were even out the door that he had won over my parents. By the time they found out that his "musical interests" were a rock 'n' roll band instead of a chamber group, they had already accepted him as my boyfriend and didn't make a fuss.

That first date was like a dream come true. I was so numb with anticipation that I didn't really feel up to talking. With the radio blaring. I couldn't have if I'd wanted to.

We went straight to the garage on the side of his folks' shingled house. Walking through the doors was like entering a make-believe land. There were posters on the walls, some of them of groups that looked almost scary with their slicked-back new-wave haircuts and black leather jackets. Incense was burning in little holders all over the place, and there were fat cushions strewn all over the cold cement floor. I thought it was pretty nice of Skip's dad to let him have the run of the garage, especially when it meant parking his own car in the driveway.

To be honest, I couldn't keep track of the

band members. None of them looked much like Skip. They seemed a lot older and tougher than he. They all smoked cigarettes and talked about knocking off early so they could go drink some beer.

If I'd been someone else, someone who wanted to be the center of attention, I wouldn't have enjoyed it all so much. But after all the guys mumbled hello, they seemed to lose interest in me (not that they'd had any to begin with) and just talked among themselves.

"Look, man, I wanna get that one riff down tonight," the bass player drawled. "And I think the changes on 'Sledgehammer' just don't make it."

I had no idea what he was saying, but I didn't care. I was part of show business, watching a band rehearse!

I didn't even mind that I couldn't get into the music. Oh, there were one or two songs I really liked. But for a girl who'd always liked bands like the Eagles, it was pretty heavy stuff. "Sledge-hammer" almost sounded like one of my father's construction sites—jarring thuds on the drums and screeching, high notes on the bass and guitars. On one song, when Skip and the bass player both played right into the amplifiers to get what they called feedback, I was afraid the top of my head was going to fly off. I knew I'd have to write some fresh stuff to show Skip the next time we got together, and I couldn't think of a single one of my poems that could possibly be set to this music.

Skip played one pretty ballad called "Starshine,"

and I thought there was a chance I could come up with something like that. I certainly wasn't the right person to write lines like: "Sledge-hammer, you've done dealt a death blow to my heart"!

When rehearsal broke up, Skip and the guys stood in a corner, laughing and talking quietly and setting up the date for another session. I wondered if he'd forgotten I was there. But when they started packing up their things and leaving, with nobody saying goodbye to me or anything like that, he walked back to where I was sitting.

"Great sounds, hey?" he asked. Then, before I could think up an answer, he slung an arm around my shoulder. "Let's head for the Hut, babe. I'm dying for some food."

"What about your parents?" I asked, wanting to be able to assure Mom and Dad I'd been introduced.

"What about them?" he asked.

"Well, don't you think you should introduce me?" I asked, hoping I didn't sound too forward.

But Skip didn't take it that way. He just looked at me as if I were crazy. "Why in the world would you ever want to meet them, Laurie?" he asked, sounding genuinely puzzled. "They're just strict and old and dull and out of it. You know, *parents*."

"But my mom and dad aren't like that," I insisted. "At least, not too much."

He shrugged. "Well, consider yourself lucky then." He jingled the car keys in his hand.

"C'mon, let's go." I dropped the subject of his parents. Maybe they were real ogres, I thought, my heart going out to him. Or maybe they were so old and doddering he was embarrassed to have me meet them. If Mom and Dad asked about Skip's family, I decided I'd just tell them the truth, that they were there all along but hadn't spent any time with us.

The Hut was mobbed by the time we got there, and this time I saw a few familiar faces. Janie Elkins' brother, Bob, was there with a girl and another couple, and he waved to Skip and called hello when we walked in. Coreen and Wes were in a booth near the front. I saw Deborah gesturing frantically at me from a booth way over on the other side. She was surrounded by a whole mob of kids who all had that preppy sort of Plainview look. I waved to her casually, as if to say I didn't think being in the Hut was such a big deal. But I knew we'd be gossiping like fiends about this by the time we saw each other Monday at lunch.

Jeff Aldridge wasn't in sight, and I felt kind of disappointed. I'd just gotten into thinking of him as a permanent fixture of the Hut, I suppose. "Where's your friend Jeff?" I asked Skip after we'd ordered ice cream sodas from a different waiter. "Doesn't he work tonight?"

"Who knows?" he said, making it clear he couldn't care less. "I don't keep tabs on him. He's just the guy who tutors me in trig. Why are you so interested, anyway?" he asked, a teasing gleam coming into his eyes. "Don't tell me you're tired of me already!"

"Of course not, silly!" I assured him, feeling that same little glow of satisfaction I'd felt the day before when he'd acted jealous. "I just figured he was here all the time."

"No way! He's probably locked in his room cracking the books or something." Skip shook his head. "Poor guy probably never has any fun," he added sarcastically. "But let's not talk about him. Let's talk about something that matters. Like, how did you like the band? And if you didn't like it," he threatened lightly, "you'd better lie 'cause I'm very sensitive."

"I don't have to lie," I said truthfully. "I don't know nearly as much about music as you do, but I thought you sounded great. You guys are really onto something."

"You think so?" His whole face lit up. "Listen, I've got some big plans for the Bonkers...."

Skip talked on and on about the group and the songs he was working on. Even though a lot of what he was saying didn't really interest me, I listened carefully because *he* was saying it and because he was sharing his hopes and his dreams with me. By the time he was done, I felt pretty committed to the Bonkers myself and could hardly wait to get home to start working up some lyrics.

I didn't have to worry about what to say, either. Skip was so energized by the rehearsal that he couldn't stop talking about it. Talk about dedication! I actually had to interrupt him at eleven to tell him I had to be getting home.

He looked up at the clock in surprise. I was

afraid he was going to make some smart remark about my folks treating me like a little kid by giving me such an early curfew, but he just said, "Sure thing. Let's get a check and go then. I gotta confess I'm beat. These rehearsals really take a lot out of me."

When he braked at the curb in front of my house and shut off the engine, I held my breath, waiting for him to kiss me. But all he did was say, "C'mon, I'll walk you to the door."

I took the smallest steps possible up the front walk, wanting to stretch every last minute of our date, knowing I'd remember every single second of this night for days to come.

I fumbled in my shoulder bag for the front door key when we reached it, not wanting to have to ring the bell. I could tell by the light streaming through the living room curtains that my parents were in there watching television.

With the key in my hand I looked up, and there was Skip, looking down at me, seeming taller than ever now that we were standing so close together. "Thursday's the only day there's no football practice after school. What do you say to going to the Hut after classes and trying to come up with some lyrics?"

"Thursday?" I hesitated, wondering if I'd be able to write something by then, something good enough to show Skip.

"Yeah, Thursday," he said real softly. Then he bent down a little and brushed his lips lightly against mine in the most romantic kiss I could have dreamed of.

"Thursday's okay." My voice came out like a little sigh. I leaned my head back for another kiss, which, when it came, was even sweeter and nicer than the first.

I waited until Skip had turned and was walking back to his car before I tried to put the key in the lock. I couldn't let him see how his kisses had made my hand tremble!

I managed to get all my school assignments done that weekend, but I had to go without sleep to do them. I was so busy trying to think of ideas to turn into songs for Skip that I didn't even begin studying until late Sunday night. Earlier I had also been busily sorting through my clothes, deciding how I could alter some things to make them look more in fashion or what to wear with what. I had also been experimenting with some new makeup I'd bought. If I'd had a good reason to look my best before, now it was even better. If I was going to be Skip Reardon's girlfriend, I'd have to be one of the slickest-looking girls in town!

We sort of eased into going steady, not dating all the time, but sneaking little meetings in the halls between classes and meeting for a few minutes after school before Skip had to go to football practice or math tutoring. It wasn't long before just about everyone at Seven Oaks knew we were a twosome. Suddenly kids who'd never paid any attention to me were stopping me in the halls to chat or yelling, "Hey, Laurie, how's it going?" every time we passed on the stairs. I had a new identity—Skip Reardon's girlfriend—and I didn't mind losing the burden of being plain Laurie Adams at all.

Now I was the leader of the lunch table! The first time Terri asked me for advice about getting a new haircut, I almost fell over, stunned that she'd ask me for help. Then I realized I had a new status—not only was I the only one in the group to have a steady boyfriend, but he was Somebody and that made me Somebody, too.

The only real problem I had at first was writing lyrics. I was so used to writing poetry that the first few songs I came up with were, in Skip's words, "from hunger."

"You've got to loosen up your style, Laurie," he told me. "The beat's the most important thing in rock music. Remember that. And keep the words simple, for gosh sakes! You've got to get rid of all these whatchamacallits you keep sticking in."

"Metaphors," I said faintly. We'd paid a lot of attention to metaphors in ninth-grade English, and I'd always been proud of being able to invent lines like "My heart's a cold, damp chamber."

The look on Skip's face told me what he thought of stuff like that. "From now on, just say what you're trying to say and don't pretty it up so much," he instructed. Then, seeing the way my face fell, his own expression softened, and he tapped gently on my forehead. "You've got a zillion great ideas up here, babe," he said in a way that made my heart skip a beat. "We'll make a songwriter out of you yet."

Music became my life. I spent every second I

could listening to the radio and to whatever albums I could afford out of my allowance. All Skip had to say was something like, "The kind of songs I really want to play are like what Springsteen's doing," and I'd be off to the record store, blowing all my money on Bruce Springsteen albums.

Didi was still hoping for a date with someone in the band, so she was more than willing to sit around playing records with me after school. That way she got two things accomplished: she learned more about the type of music the Bonkers were playing, and she got more chances to nag me about fixing her up with one of Skip's friends.

"Tell me again what they look like," she pleaded one afternoon when we were sitting around at her house, playing a bunch of Coreen's albums on her stereo.

I groaned. "Didi, I've described them all at least five times! And I've told you, I don't really know any of them. I've only been to two rehearsals. Skip says the guys get nervous when someone's watching them practice."

"Ummmm." Her eyes closed tightly, and her face screwed up with such concentration that I could almost see the parade of their imagined faces passing through her mind. "I think I want to meet the bass player. He's the one you said was skinny with dark hair, right?"

"Okay, okay," I said, knowing I'd have to at least try, or she'd never talk to me again. "I'll ask Skip if we can double-date with Lenny and you one night."

"Lenny?" She made a sort of tsk-tsking sound with her lips. "Gee, that's not a very rock star sort of name, is it?"

"Look, Didi"—my patience was going fast, and I had to keep my voice even and low so she wouldn't know—"do you want to go out with a boy or a name? Should I just forget about saying anything to Skip?"

"No, no, no! I want to go out with Len, honest. I mean, Len doesn't sound as yucky as Lenny, does it?" She hurried on. "Sure, Laurie, ask Skip if you can fix me up with Len. Or someone else in the group if Len's got a girl already. There's going to be a revival of *Woodstock* at the Strand next weekend, so maybe we can go see that. You *will* ask him, won't you?"

She looked so desperate I almost felt sorry for her. If our places were changed, I knew I'd probably be nagging Didi to get *me* a date with one of her boyfriend's buddies. "Cross my heart, Didi. Next time I talk to him, I'll ask him. Now, where's that old David Bowie album? Skip says there's a cut on it I've just got to hear."

Those first few weeks with Skip went by so quickly that I really didn't have much time to think about our relationship, and frankly, I didn't try. I liked the feeling of having been swept off my feet. After all, I was Somebody now. That was good enough for me.

It wasn't good enough for Mom and Dad, though. I could tell by the way Mom would sometimes murmur, "Are you going out with

Skip again tonight, Laurie? Don't you think you should see some other boys, too?"

When I was in a super-good mood, I'd turn remarks like that into jokes, with a snappy comeback like, "As soon as someone else asks me out, I'll go!" When I was touchy, I'd come right out and say, "I don't want to see anyone else." And when I was afraid she might order me not to go steady with Skip, I'd pretend I hadn't heard her and not say a word.

Actually, I had plenty to worry about without dwelling on the problem of what to do if some other boy did ask me out (and that wasn't much of a problem since every other guy at Seven Oaks seemed to know I was going with Skip). For one thing, I worried about staying pretty enough and hip enough to keep Skip interested when I knew there was plenty of competition from girls just dying to take him away from me.

I wasn't the kind of girl who'd go all the way sexually to keep a boyfriend, and fortunately Skip never pressured me for more than kissing and cuddling. But there was a lot more to that in keeping a guy interested, and I knew it. Soon I was so educated about rock music that I could keep up with anything Skip was saying about the music world, even if he was talking about something that didn't really interest me, like, "Iggy Pop's really gotten his act together."

Without bothering to explain that I couldn't understand why anyone would like Iggy Pop's music, I'd say, "He sure got a great write-up in *Rolling Stone* last month."

I was always figuring out ways to make money to buy new clothes so I'd be one of the best-dressed girls at Seven Oaks. Nights when Skip was being tutored or playing at a job with the band, I'd babysit in the neighborhood. Afternoons when he had football practice or a rehearsal, I'd run errands for the neighbors or rake their lawns.

With all the new activities to keep me busy, I had to stay up late nearly every night to get any of my homework done. I'd turn on the little night light next to my bed so Mom and Dad wouldn't know what late hours I was keeping, but even so, they caught me more than once.

"What in the world are you doing up at one o'clock in the morning?" Mom asked, her voice sharp with worry, when she walked into my room one night. "Are you sick?"

"No, just not sleepy," I lied, widening my eyes so she couldn't guess I was having trouble keeping them open. I tried the defensive tactic, "What are *you* doing up?"

"Watching a late movie. Not that that's got anything to do with the question, young lady. You're the growing girl who needs her sleep." She frowned, then walked over to the bed and removed my biology book from my hand. "Go to sleep, Laurie," she said, setting the book on the table. She turned to leave, then stopped. "You're not reading your schoolbooks at night because you neglect your work during the day, I hope?"

"Oh, no. Of course not. I just couldn't get to sleep, so I thought I may as well read."

"Well, turn out the light and go to bed now,"

she said, not sounding too convinced. "I'm sure you'll fall asleep if you lie down and close your eyes."

After that, I was careful not to stay up late too often, but that made it even harder to find time to study. Sometimes I even read from a propped-open book while I was jamming my electric rollers in my hair.

It's not surprising I was getting more and more tired. Some days I looked so dead to the world, I had to put on twice as much blusher to get any color into my cheeks. But I didn't worry about any of it—not even when I fell asleep in English class and would have gotten caught if the guy in back of me hadn't suddenly crossed his feet, hitting my chair and jolting me awake.

How could I worry? After all, I was on cloud nine. Besides, hadn't all those books and poems I'd read while I was waiting to start really living prepared me for this? Being in love was wonderful, I guess, but it could sure wear a girl out.

Chapter Twelve

By the time I came up with some lyrics that Skip was enthusiastic about, I really felt as if I'd been through the mill. I had spent an entire month writing one song after another. Each time, all my hard work would be rewarded by Skip's turning up his nose and telling me, "This is supposed to be a rock song, Laurie, not some Pulitzer Prize-winning poem! It's just not my kind of song, babe."

The more disappointed I was, the more determined I became to write something he really went for—and the more scared that if I didn't come up with something soon, he'd start looking for a girl who was more on his wavelength.

And then I did it.

My newest lyrics carefully tucked inside my notebook, I'd met Skip after school to go to the Hut. I was so worried that he'd hate them that I couldn't bring myself to tell him about them until we'd parked.

Even then, I couldn't say anything. "Here," I blurted, thrusting the folded paper at him. "See what you think."

He didn't say a word, just unfolded the page and started reading. I waited, holding my breath, not wanting to look at him in case his reaction was the usual frown of discouragement. I whistled under my breath, stared at the minute hand sweeping around the dashboard clock, and fiddled with the cigarette lighter.

I was staring into space when Skip suddenly shifted around in the driver's seat, leaned over, and gave me a hug so hard it hurt my ribs. "What's the matter?" I gulped. "Is something wrong?"

"Wrong? Nothing could be righter, Laurie. This is terrific! You've really got it! I'm proud of you, babe."

I blushed and giggled, embarrassed now that

I was finally getting some praise for my work. I sagged back against the cushions of the car as the awful built-up tension drained out of me. "You mean it, Skip?" I asked, still not willing to believe my ears. "You really like it?"

He held the paper in front of him, his eyes scanning the words through once more before he answered. "Like it? I love it!" he said, his voice ringing. I felt as happy as if he'd said he loved *me*.

"Do you think it'll be hard for you to come up with a melody?" I asked, trying hard to remain professional, which wasn't easy since I was ready to faint from sheer relief. I knew full well that what I'd come up with was more than a bunch of words for a song. I'd come up with what I needed to hold Skip's interest, to make him realize he'd made the right choice with me.

"As a matter of fact," he said, not making the slightest attempt to keep from gloating, "I think I've got a rough idea of how it's going to sound already. Want to hear it?"

Did I want to hear my lyrics coming out of his lips? No one ever wanted anything more! I was so beside myself with joy I could only nod my head, feeling the flush creep up and across my cheekbones as he started singing in a low, husky voice. I'd called it "Shelter in the Storm." I'd written the song just for him, and now he was singing it just for me.

> *The world's so big*
> *That I can't help feeling lost.*
> *People fighting for themselves,*
> *Never thinking of the cost.*

But I know I'll get by
If you're by my side.
And I know in your arms
I'll find someplace to hide.

You're the one
Who makes my world so safe and bright.
You're my beacon, you're my light.
You're the one.
When you're near in every way,
I'm not afraid to face each day.
Yes, you're the one,
You are my shelter in the storm.

I act brave,
But at times I feel so small.
That's when I need you most of all.
With your love,
I know I'm gonna be all right,
Every day and every night,
Because . . .

You're the one.
Who makes my world so safe and bright.
You're my beacon, you're my light.
You're the one.
When you're near in every way,
I'm not afraid to face each day.
Yes, you're my shelter in the storm.

Tears came to my eyes as he sang. "Oh, Skip, you make it sound so beautiful!" I whispered when he'd finished.

"It *is* beautiful," he said simply. "I'm sorry I told you you were being too poetic. This song is sheer poetry, Laurie, but it works, it really

works. You're wonderful, babe," he murmured
in my ear, leaning across the seat to plant a
little kiss on my temple. "You really *are* my
shelter in the storm."

I could have burst into tears. It was all so
wonderful and romantic!

"I'm so happy, Skip," I whispered, feeling safe
and secure in the shelter in his arms. "I hope
we can write lots more together."

He held me a little away from him and gazed
down at me with those wonderful blue eyes of
his. "I think we're a great new team," he said
softly before his lips met mine. "It's not every
day a guy meets a chick who cares about music
as much as he does."

Then there was nothing left but the kissing,
which made me feel so good and close to him
that it even managed to make me feel all right
about fooling him. What would he think if he
found out that my taste in music was really
light years away from his—or that music wasn't
at all what *my* world revolved around? Still, my
world revolved around *him*, and that was enough
to keep me writing songs to make him happy.

It took a real effort to pull myself away from
him. "Hey!" I laughed happily, the joy rushing
to the surface from someplace deep inside. "Don't
forget we're practically in a public place."

He laughed, too, looking out the window as if
he were just remembering we were parked along
the street. "So we are! C'mon, let's go real
public and celebrate. Anything on the menu is
yours today."

So we walked into the Hut, hand in hand, the

perfect couple at last. I thought nothing could spoil this incredible day. But no sooner were we seated at "our" booth than Jeff Aldridge had to come up and ruin everything.

"How're you guys doing?" he asked, coming up to take our order. But before either one of us could answer, he casually said to Skip, "I've got to talk to you about yesterday's trig exam before you leave."

The hostile look Skip had started getting on his face whenever Jeff Aldridge was around lately showed up, making his features look mean instead of angelic. "If you've got something to say, say it!"

Jeff seemed nervous. He shifted his weight from one foot to the other. "Hey, man, lighten up. I just think maybe we should talk about it alone," he said in a low voice.

"Anything you've got to say to me, Laurie can hear. After all," he said, biting off each word, "she *is* my girlfriend. We don't have any secrets from each other, do we, hon?"

"No." I shook my head, my eyes glued to Jeff. What could be wrong? Jeff always seemed overflowing with self-confidence and warmth, but now he was acting so awkward.

"You flunked," he said, just like that, and I realized that the dirty look he was aiming at Skip wasn't because of the way Skip had acted as much as because Skip had made him say it in front of me.

"I didn't even want to tell you this, but Coach O'Brien's making me. He got the results from Mr. Morris today." Jeff paused. "And believe me, you're better off hearing this from me than from Coach O'Brien. He's benching you for next week's game. And if you don't do better on the next big test, he's dropping you from the team for good." Jeff looked so sad, you'd have thought he was the one being put on football probation. "I'm really sorry, Skip. I did what I could to help, but—well, I'd really thought you'd studied for this one."

"Yeah, well—" Skip shrugged, then slowly stood up so he was just a few inches from Jeff. When he spoke again, his voice sounded a little threatening. "No big deal, Aldridge. You know what I mean? I've been meaning to tell you anyway that I think I study better on my own. I'll talk to the coach about dropping tutoring so you don't have to waste your valuable time any more." He looked down at me, then jerked his head. "Come on, Laurie, let's split."

I pulled my coat on slowly, then stood up, avoiding Jeff's hurt, puzzled eyes as he walked away. I almost started trying to explain to Skip that Jeff had only been trying to be nice, but the set expression on his face kept me quiet. When I watched him reach down and pick up the sheet of lyrics, folding it into a small square and tucking it in his jacket pocket, I felt pretty mad at Jeff myself. There I'd been, having the most special experience of my life—and he'd had to come along and ruin it.

All the way to my house, Skip was silent as a tomb. I was afraid to say a word. No matter how much he tried to act as if he didn't care, I knew he had to be upset about being benched. All

Skip's father had talked about, when I finally met him, was the importance of a college education and what an incredible sport football was. I knew Skip was in trouble.

By the time we got to my house, Skip's anger seemed gone, but I could tell by the droop of his shoulders and the dead tone in his voice that the real depression was setting in. "Well, I'd better go home," he said, his voice so loud after that long silence that I could hear the effort he was making to sound casual.

"Are you sure you don't want to come in?" I asked, trying to sound as if nothing horrible had happened. "Mom made some of those applesauce cookies you like yesterday."

"No, babe." In the dim light, I could see him shake his head sadly. "I guess I should go face the old man right away. Boy, is he going to be ticked off!"

I wanted to throw my arms around him, but his voice was so shaky I was afraid he'd cry if I did, then hate me for causing it. So I just reached over and squeezed his shoulder. "Give me a call later?" I asked.

"Yeah, sure." He swiveled around and gave me a quick kiss. "And don't worry," he added, more in his normal tone of voice, "Aldridge didn't make me forget about our song. By this time next week, I'll have it ready, and you can hear the band play it."

As I walked to the house, I knew that for once, something mattered more to Skip than his music. I only hoped he managed to do well on the next test.

But it was worse than I thought. When Skip called after dinner, I had to hold the receiver away from my ear more than once because he was shouting more than talking.

"I can't believe it! If I had more money saved up, I'd just pack up and get out right now!" he yelled. "I just wish my father had to go through being young all over again so maybe he could remember how it feels!"

"Was it that bad?" I asked stupidly.

"Bad?" He was nearly shrieking. "How about not being allowed to use the car or to go out except for school and important gigs? Do you call that bad?"

My heart felt as if it were zooming all the way down to the tips of my toes. "You—you mean we can't see each other?" I mumbled. "Not at all?"

He laughed, but it sounded more like a sob. "Don't worry about that, babe. We'll figure out a way to get around *that*. But we sure won't be able to see as much of each other as usual. Oh, God, Laurie, why did they ever have to invent trigonometry?"

"Don't worry," I said, wishing I could think of something more comforting. "All you have to do is really study hard and get a good grade the next time, and your father will forget all about this grade."

"Oh, I'm not worried about *that*, believe me. There's no way I'm going to get anything but a good grade on the next exam. It's just the three weeks in between I'm nuts about. My mom and dad aren't even letting me rehearse with the band because they say it takes up too much time. Out of the goodness of his heart, the old man's allowing me an hour every night to practice guitar by myself. Real big of him!"

I was pretty sure that if I'd failed a big test, my folks wouldn't allow me even that, but I didn't think this was the time to tell Skip that. Instead, I did my best to cheer him up, saying "You'll probably be a great solo guitarist by the time you're done."

"Yeah, maybe you're right." He sounded tired all of a sudden, as if his anger had used up all his energy. "Look, Laurie, I'm not even supposed to be on the phone except to call the guys and cancel rehearsals, so I'd better get off. I'll be able to meet you for just a few minutes after school tomorrow, okay?"

"Okay," I agreed. "Parking lot door?"

"You got it, babe. And don't forget," he added, trying to make a joke of the whole thing, "this is my storm, but *you* are my shelter."

"You bet I am!" I meant every word of it.

Since Skip usually had football practice in the mornings as well as in the afternoons, I'd never stopped taking the school bus with Didi. The next day, I could hardly wait to get to her house. I really needed to talk to someone about what had happened, and I could hardly be expected to go running to my mom and tell her that my boyfriend with the "promising future" was practically flunking out of school.

But to my surprise, Didi didn't seem especially upset about it. I don't know why I'd expected her to understand. She'd been less adoring of

Skip ever since I'd had to tell her that *all* the guys in his band had steadies. I think, too, she'd put the blame on him for my not going out for Glee Club with her, even though she'd never had a chance of getting in with her off-key voice.

"It's only three weeks or so, Laurie," she said calmly, reminding me a lot of my mother when I used to moan and groan about how I couldn't wait for Christmas or my birthday to arrive.

"But three weeks is forever! And I'll be all by myself. Oh, Didi, what am I going to do?"

"It's not forever, and you won't be all by yourself," she reminded me as we were climbing onto the bus. "Or don't you count your friends as company?"

That got to me, since I knew I'd been spending a lot less time with her since I'd starting seeing Skip. "Of course I count my friends. What would I do without you?"

"How about what you can do with me?" she asked, giving me a questioning look.

"I don't know what you mean."

"Do I have to spell it out? Now that you won't be tied up either seeing Mr. Reardon or scribbling songs for him night and day, you'll have plenty of time to go to the Hut with me after school."

"The Hut?" I was in shock. I couldn't picture myself going in there without Skip.

"Sure, why not?" she said, making it sound like the most sensible idea in the world. "I really don't like going with Deborah whenever she's got a ride. Those Plainview juniors are a drag, and, besides, there're always too many people in that crowd to be able to have a good time. We can go together while Skip's grounded."

She said it as if it were already settled, and for the life of me, I couldn't think of any argument against going. There was no reason I should sit home for three weeks just because Skip had screwed up. I told myself I was positive he'd want me to have a good time while he was shut up at home—as long as I didn't flirt with other guys, that is. And I had no intention of doing that. So I told Didi I'd go with her sometime. "When do you want to go?" I asked.

"Why not this afternoon?"

I sighed. Didi wouldn't want to hear how much homework I had to do, assignments that were already overdue, not when she'd rubbed it in about how much I'd been ignoring her lately. "Sure," I told her as the bus turned into the school parking lot. "Why not?"

Chapter Thirteen

Didi was practically bouncing up and down at lunchtime. Even though she didn't mention the Hut because she didn't want the other girls to know we were going, I knew that was the reason for her high spirits. I wished I could feel as eager about going there as she did. But Skip's punishment had put a cloud over everything. Nobody asked anything when I didn't volunteer any information about it, but I was aware of Terri, Deborah, and Gerry, another former Plainview girl, giving me odd looks all the time we were eating, and I knew they were just dying to know how I felt. But I was so depressed by the whole thing that I didn't want to discuss it with any of them.

The more I thought about it, the more going to the Hut seemed like a good idea, even though it meant taking the public bus to get there. I knew I'd just feel more depressed if I went straight home and tried to write another song or read a book. I was beginning to understand the old saying, "Misery loves company."

Speaking of misery, Skip wasn't exactly overflowing with good spirits when I met him by the parking lot door after school. I'd already told Didi that I'd meet her by the front door after I saw him. I wasn't planning to keep my trip to the Hut from him, but when I did tell him, I planned to hedge a little and say I'd run into Didi and gone with her on the spur of the moment.

As I walked down the corridor after the last bell and spied Skip's lean form slouched against the wall, my heart went out to him. His shoulders still seemed bowed in defeat. I was flattered to see how happily he smiled when he saw me. Maybe his punishment would make him appreciate me all the more, I reasoned.

"I've only got a couple of minutes, hon." He shifted his stack of books to rest on one hip and bent down to kiss me quickly on the cheek.

"Feel any better?" I asked, worried at the stony look in his eyes and sensing some new kind of attitude in him, one I was afraid was more stubborn than optimistic.

"Nah, not really," he said sulkily, frowning. "But there's not much I can do about it, so I may as well grin and bear it." To illustrate his point, he crossed his eyes and grinned hideously.

"Didn't your mother ever tell you your eyes would stay that way?" I scolded teasingly, giving him a little jab in the ribs.

"You kidding? All my mother ever told me was to get good grades so I could go to some stupid college." He banged the door hard with his fist. "I'll show her who can get good grades! Then she'll have no right to complain about my music again!"

What could I say? Skip didn't appear to be in any mood to be consoled, and his martyred saint act was starting to wear a little thin. After all, he was the one who'd goofed off and failed the math test. If he was so determined to kiss off his high school diploma, it seemed he ought to be more grown up about accepting the punishment. But I was afraid to lecture him if it might worsen his black mood. So I just leaned there against the wall, tracing little circles on the grimy paint with my free hand and bouncing my books against my thigh with the other.

"Hey, I'm gonna work on our song tonight," Skip said halfheartedly.

"Great." I felt about as enthusiastic as he sounded. It was with a terrible shock that I realized I was bored. Me bored with Skip? That was a laugh, I thought. I was just too self-involved and selfish to care about what he was going through. Blaming myself made me want to be nicer to him, so I gave him my sweetest smile and hooked my arm through his. "When will I get to hear it?"

"I'm hoping my folks'll soften up a little and let me come over to your house one night to play it. I can't bring the band, but it might still be nice. You know, to let your folks hear it and all."

"That's a wonderful idea, Skip!" I said, already picturing how proud I'd be to have Mom and Dad hear the song we'd written together.

"Yeah, well, maybe next week. I'll let you know." He flipped his wrist up and looked at his digital watch. "I'd better go. Boy, I'll bet my dad's really getting his jollies treating me like a kid! He even made up a chart, and I have to sign in and out every day." He snorted. "Like being in prison."

"I guess I won't see you over the weekend, but call if you can, all right? I'll miss you," I whispered.

"I'll miss you, too, Laurie." He stopped as he was going out the door and turned around. "Not going to the game?"

"No. Since you're not playing—"

"You should go, Laurie. Really. I know I'd give anything to be there, even on the sidelines," he said, and the agony in his voice told me for the very first time that Skip actually cared about football. "If you change your mind and do go, think of me. And write down any big plays so you can tell me about them," he added as he went out the door.

"Well, all right," I said, more to please him than anything else. Actually, I hated football. I went to the games only because Skip was on the team. It was expected of me.

Didi was already waiting in front of the school, hiding in the shadows by the main doors and reading the notices on the bulletin board so she wouldn't look like she was waiting for someone. "It's about time!" she grumbled when I walked up to her.

"School's only been out ten minutes, dodo!" I reminded her. "And I already told you I had to meet Skip."

"How's Mr. Math Genius? Off to hit the old books and slide rule?"

"Funny, Didi!" I said sharply. "Real funny! I suppose we can wait to hear your name being read in the honor roll at the big assembly next month?"

That one got to her. As a matter of fact, it shut her up so quickly I had an idea her grades were worse than I'd thought. "C'mon." I pushed the doors open. "Let's get out of here."

We didn't talk much on the bus, since I was sort of hurt about Didi's making a joke out of something that was so serious to me. She seemed lost in her own daydreams. She was probably wondering if anyone would pay attention to her at the Hut.

But by the time we got off the bus, I was worried about how I'd be greeted. After all, Jeff knew what had happened with Skip and the math test even if nobody else did. I wouldn't be surprised if he was able to put two and two together and come up with the answer that I was alone because Skip was in big trouble with his folks.

I stood up straight and pushed my shoulders back as we walked into the Hut. Let Jeff make fun of Skip if he wanted to! Not everyone could get A's without trying, and Jeff might be a brain, but he couldn't play guitar like Skip could! I was so keyed up by the time we found a booth that it was lucky for Jeff he hadn't started yet, or I might have done something we'd both have been sorry for.

"Where's your friend?" Didi asked me after we'd ordered from Dolly. "You know, the cute one with the adorable freckles on his nose, Skip's buddy?"

"Who knows?" I answered, using the same words Skip had when I'd asked him about Jeff. "He's not such a great friend of Skip's anymore." I didn't mention I'd never noticed his freckles, but I made a little mental note to check and see if Didi was right.

I got my chance in about half an hour. I saw Jeff as he came through the door, but when he went to catch my eye, I turned away and started talking to Didi, smiling broadly, as if I didn't have a care in the world. I didn't know why I was blaming Jeff, but I felt as if it was all his fault Skip was confined to his house.

I was so obvious about it that Jeff had to have guessed I was ignoring him on purpose. He walked on the other side of the room, by the counter, to the back room to change into his waiter's clothes. When he was working on the floor, he seemed to be making a point of avoiding our table. Didi finally had to wave at him to get his attention so she could order a second vanilla Coke.

"Hi, you're Didi, right?" he said brightly, and I understood why he made Skip so crazy. Leave it to Jeff Aldridge to remember Didi's name after only meeting her once! Maybe he remembered her because he liked her, I thought, but that didn't make me feel any friendlier toward him.

I thought he was going to snub me, but I should have known better. Jeff really was too mature to do that. "How's everything, Laurie?" he asked, and his voice was so worried, so caring that it was hard for me to stay mad.

Nevertheless, I did. "I'm fine, thanks," I said icily. "I'll have another Coke, too, please, a plain one."

He looked at me strangely, but didn't say a word then or when he brought over our drinks. As I thought about it, I felt small and nasty for the way I was treating him. As soon as Didi went to play the jukebox or to go to the girls' room, I decided, I'd call him over and apologize for being so obnoxious.

He must have been waiting for her to leave, too, because as soon as she got up from the booth and headed back to the restroom to fix her makeup, he walked over.

"How's Skip?" he asked. He wasn't gloating or acting triumphant but sounded concerned.

"I called him last night to find out how his folks took the news, but he said he didn't feel like talking."

"I'm not surprised he didn't want to talk to you," I said bitterly, my urge to apologize quickly forgotten. "How would you feel if you'd been grounded for three weeks?"

He let out a long whistle. "They really came down hard, didn't they? But I don't know why Skip's mad at *me*, Laurie. I didn't ask to tutor him, you know, but I tried my best to help him pass the test. And he could have, too, if he'd just studied a little more."

"That's easy for you to say!"

"Easy? What makes you think I've got it so easy? Look, Laurie, I have to work just as hard as anyone else to get good grades, maybe even harder because I've got a job, too. And it's important for me to do well because the only way I'm going to get to college is if I get a scholarship. I couldn't afford it otherwise—and I want to go to college."

"You know, there's a lot more to life than school," I said scornfully.

"Yeah, I know." He laughed. "And I try to do it all—go out for sports, keep my grades up, practice piano, and go out sometimes with the gang, too."

"You play piano?" I just about barked the words, I was so stunned.

"Yeah. Since I was ten years old. Oh, I'm not in Skip's league or anything. I used to play once in a while with the school dance band, but my grades started slipping, so I gave that up."

Suddenly he looked serious. "You can't do *everything* and still graduate with decent grades, Laurie. It was hard for me to learn, but I did. I hope Skip realizes it now, too."

"Don't worry," I assured him coldly. "Skip has every intention of getting an A on the next test."

"Well, I hope so. You know, you could help him out by encouraging him to spend more time on his schoolwork. It probably wouldn't hurt your own grades, either."

"I happen to be a straight-A student!" I snapped. "I always have been. I think you have a lot of nerve talking to me like this."

"Whoa, whoa!" He put his hands up as if to fend off imaginary blows. "Hey, I wasn't trying to insult you. You just don't act like a girl who's serious about school, that's all. I'm glad I'm wrong."

"Should I go away and come back again?" Didi asked in a low, nervous voice. "Looks like I'm interrupting something."

"Not at all," I told her, turning away from Jeff without even a smile. "We've said all we had to say."

I refused to tell Didi what Jeff and I were talking about, knowing she'd figure it was about Skip. I started telling her all about my new song instead. As soon as I could do it without her guessing something was wrong, I said it was time for me to leave.

How dare Jeff Aldridge lecture me, I thought as I was walking from the bus stop to my house. I kicked a pebble and sent it flying across the street. I couldn't believe he'd chalked me up as a dummy, somebody who wasn't serious about school. The worst part was that he wasn't that far from wrong. I'd been so busy with makeup, clothes, and my new boyfriend this year that I was constantly late handing in my assignments and was seeing more C's than A's inked across the tops of my test papers and essays. But that still didn't mean I was silly or dumb.

I tried to put the whole thing out of my mind, but it wasn't easy. That night, instead of going to the football game, I decided to study. The truth of how much I'd let my grades slip really hit home, especially when I pulled out all my English quizzes and saw that I'd received only one A out of nine tests. I'd been pushing all the B and C papers into my notebook and forgetting about them, but when I saw them all spread out in front of me in black and white, I began to see that maybe Jeff was right.

You know, I actually enjoyed that weekend without Skip more than I would have believed. I sat around and watched TV with Mom and Dad instead of cooping myself up with my stereo and record albums. When I wasn't studying, I read the Kurt Vonnegut book that had just come out in paperback and that I'd been dying to read ever since I'd seen it listed on the English class reading list. Since I spent the entire weekend at home, inside or helping Mom in the garden, I didn't even bother putting on makeup or setting my hair.

When Skip called me Sunday night to complain he was going stir crazy, I couldn't feel sorry for him. "Why don't you just try to make the best of it?" I suggested. "I've been home all weekend myself, and I don't feel like a prisoner."

"That's just because you know you could go out if you wanted to," he insisted. Then, maybe catching on that I was losing sympathy with his moaning, he said, "But let's not talk about it any more. I was actually phoning to tell you my folks said I could come over to your house this week for an hour or two to play our song for your parents, as long as I don't go anywhere else. What do you say? If you want, you could invite your aunt and uncle, and we'll have a real premier performance!"

"Oh, Skip, that'll be terrific!" I forgot my irritation, too excited at the prospect of showing him off to Aunt Mary and Uncle Don. "I'll check it out with everyone and let you know tomorrow at school which night's best, okay? I'm sure Mom will invite you for dinner—and maybe your folks can come, too."

"Forget that, babe. I've seen too much of *them* lately as it is. But I'm sure they won't make a fuss about me staying for dinner. I could play the song afterward."

"I can hardly wait! I'll talk to Mom right now."

My parents and Aunt Mary and Uncle Don all said Wednesday night was good. "And I'm glad I'm finally going to meet Skip." Mary said warmly when I called to invite her. "I'm sure he's pretty special if you're so crazy about him."

When I went to bed that night, my head was

whirling, trying to figure out what to wear Wednesday evening so Skip and I would make the perfect couple. With a start, I realized it was the first time all weekend that the thought of clothes had entered my mind.

Chapter Fourteen

My anticipation of Wednesday's dinner didn't keep me from deciding to go to the Hut with Didi on Tuesday. I almost said I couldn't when she asked me. But I realized I was reluctant only because I wanted silly Jeff Aldridge to think I was at home poring over my textbooks. Why should I care what he thought? Besides, he'd already written me off as somebody who cared only about fun. That made me so mad I almost wanted to flaunt my goofing off at him.

I really didn't want to have any secrets from Skip, but when I saw him between classes on Monday, I'd deliberately "neglected" to tell him that I'd been at "our" hangout—or that I'd made plans to go again. I reassured myself that I was keeping the truth from him for his own sake, since he'd just feel worse if he knew I was going out while he was stuck at home.

I braced myself to be snubbed Tuesday afternoon when Jeff came in to work. To my surprise, he came right to the table where Didi and

I were sitting with Deborah (who'd come with that bunch of juniors from Plainview but was sitting with us) and gave us all a big hello.

Of course, Didi was all smiles, practically gushing all over him—even though five minutes before she'd been going on about how Barry Knox had finally asked her to go to the movies with him that weekend. Deborah piped right up, too, introducing herself and flirting like a femme fatale out of a bad movie. She told Jeff in a cutesy little voice, "Of course I know who *you* are already. You're the best waiter here."

Naturally, he smiled at the fuss they made over him, but I could tell by the way his ears started turning pink that he was also a little embarrassed by it. Who wouldn't have been?

Of course, all the time they were flattering him, I could have been part of the bad paint job on the wood of the seat back. It took all my strength to pull the muscles of my face upward into something I hoped at least resembled a smile, but I was determined that Jeff Aldridge should know I had my pride. If he was going to snub me, I'd be darned if he knew it mattered!

But he didn't walk away without talking to me, after all. It even seemed as if his smile grew broader and brighter when Didi and Deborah finally stopped for air, and he shifted his attention to me on the other side of the table.

"How are you?" he asked, sounding as if he really cared. "Feeling a little better about what happened?"

"About what happened?" I murmured vaguely,

even though I knew perfectly well what he was talking about. "Oh, Skip's bad luck! Sooner or later everyone takes a test they aren't ready for. He'll do better next time."

"And how about you?" he asked, looking straight at me in a way that made my face feel suddenly hot. "You weren't lonesome all weekend?"

"Not at all," I said in the coolest tone I could muster up. "I'd been waiting for a quiet weekend so I could read the new Vonnegut book."

"Oh? I like him, too," he said in the same tone, but I had a funny feeling from the way a smile quivered on his lips that he thought I'd said it just to impress him. In a way I was disgusted with myself—because I had.

Why in the world was I acting as if Jeff Aldridge might think I didn't even know how to read? Every time he talked to me, I said something ridiculous and made a fool of myself. But it was all his fault for making me feel I had to prove myself to him! "If you're starting work, waiter, we could use another round of Cokes," I told him curtly, in an attempt to hide my self-disgust.

"Sure, that's right, isn't it? I'm just the waiter!" It was the first time I'd ever heard him sound disturbed, and I felt cold all over when I saw that he was glaring at me with just as much dislike as I'd aimed toward him. But before I could say something to turn it all into a joke or anything, he'd turned on his heel and stormed away.

"What's wrong with *you*?" Didi's eyes were

bugged out in astonishment. "That's the crummiest thing I've ever heard you say, Laurie."

"What did I do?" I asked angrily, although I knew exactly what I had done and felt sick to my stomach about it. "All I did was ask him for some more Cokes."

I looked at them with innocence written all over my face, but it didn't work. Deborah was staring at me as if she'd seen something she didn't like. "But, Laurie," she said quietly, "if you had to work after school and wait on your friends, would you want them to keep reminding you of it?"

"Look, Deborah," I snarled, "what do you know about having to work? You're rich!"

"Why don't you talk to me when you've calmed down, Laurie?" she said angrily. She stood up stiffly. "I don't know what's gotten into you, but I'm sure you're saying things you don't mean."

I stared stonily into my empty Coke glass until she was gone, sure I'd start blubbering if I tried to talk. Whatever had made me say such a nasty, stupid thing to her?

Then it was Didi's turn. "What *is* the matter, Laurie?" she asked. "It's not like you to be so mean. You know Deborah was right—you insulted Jeff." She shook her head. "It's just not like you."

"I know, I know." I bit my lip. "It's just that I'm upset about what happened to Skip, I guess."

"Do you really think that's all?"

"Of course that's all!" I took a deep breath, then lowered my voice. "Look, I was wrong, and I'll tell Jeff and Deborah I'm sorry, okay?"

As if I'd conjured him up, Jeff appeared with our Cokes. "I'm sorry if I was unfriendly," I mumbled, not able to meet his eyes. "I guess I'm not in as good a mood as I thought."

"That's okay, Laurie," he said, and when I looked up, he was smiling a little even though he still looked kind of hurt. "I know you've got a lot on your mind."

What mind? Since when do you think I've got a mind? That's what I felt like saying. What I really said was nothing. I just smiled apologetically before he walked away again. If he never spoke to me again, I thought miserably, I wouldn't blame him.

"Look," I said to Didi, "I'll go tell Deborah I'm sorry now, too, okay?"

"Do whatever you want, Laurie. It's none of my business how you treat your friends." I didn't think she was impressed with my half-hearted apology to Jeff.

It was awful, but somehow I propelled myself across the room to Deborah's table and took her aside to apologize. Thank goodness, she didn't make a big thing of it. "That's all right," she assured me. "I know what you're going through." When my jaw dropped in amazement, she added, "It's no secret about Skip being grounded, Laurie. I think it's really a drag for you, too, when you were just starting to really go steady." She gave my arm a sisterly squeeze.

I sank back down in the booth across from Didi, my mind spinning. Everyone took it for granted I was being rude and hysterical because I missed Skip. But was I? As moody as I was feeling, I realized I didn't miss Skip all that much. Was I already falling out of love with him?

"There! Everything's straightened out," I announced, doing my best to sound normal. "Should we get something to eat?"

But Didi still had that faraway expression on her face. "I've got to get home," she said. "Skip's flunking that test made me realize how lucky I was to be passing everything. I've got a lot of catching up to do."

"Me, too," I said eagerly, glad we'd found a safe subject to talk about. "You know, this weekend, I got out all my tests and looked over them, and would you believe..." But I let my voice trail off. Didi wasn't listening. She was already buttoning up her coat and signaling to Jeff for a check. I realized that she didn't feel like being with me. When Jeff dropped off the bill, his smile—detached now instead of warm— made me feel even worse. At the rate I was going, I wouldn't have a single friend left by the time Skip passed his next trig test!

I was glad, as I rode the bus home with Didi in silence, that I had Wednesday night to look forward to.

But when Skip showed up at my house that night with his guitar, it didn't turn out the way I'd dreamed it would.

Aunt Mary arrived first, looking as perky and vibrant as ever, even though the baby was due within the next month and a half. "It's a good thing I took my leave of absence when I did," she remarked. "I've become so bulky I don't think I could even slip between the lab shelves, much less sit on a stool hunched over a microscope!"

"You've never looked better in your life, and you know it," Dad corrected her.

"And I guess I'm not the only one who's looking great these days," Mary said as Don came through the door. "Or haven't you noticed that your daughter's blossomed into a real beauty? You look fabulous, Laurie. Is it Seven Oaks High or this terrific guy I've been hearing so much about?"

I could feel myself flushing, and I did my best to smile mysteriously. "Oh, I don't know. Both, I guess. Anyway, you'll be meeting Skip soon. I hope you like him."

"And your song, too, right?" Don chimed in. "I didn't know you had all this budding talent as a lyricist."

"Writings songs isn't much different from writing poetry," I explained. "I just thought it would be fun to try something new."

"Especially when there's a cute young musician in the picture, no?" Mary teased.

"Well, that helps," I admitted, and was rewarded with an understanding smile. At least Mary wasn't like Mom. She was still young enough to remember that when a girl finds the right boy for her, there's no reason to experiment with anybody else. The prickly doubts I was beginning to have about whether Skip was Mr. Right were, I was sure, just part of some silly phase I was going through. I had to smile at myself when the doorbell rang and I got up to let Skip in. Two months ago I'd been petrified that I'd *never* have a boyfriend—and now here I was, practically dissatisfied with the most fantastic guy in the entire school!

"Hi, Miss Shelter!" With one hand Skip tilted up my chin for a quick kiss. With the other hand he was carrying a guitar case and a folder of sheet music, what he called his charts.

"Well, how does it feel to be free for a little while?" I asked, knowing I was running my words together and talking too fast to cover up my nervousness. I wanted Mary to like Skip. I'd just curl up and die if he spent the whole dinner complaining about school or whining about his strict parents.

But the way he grinned and flicked his shining curls out of his face were a good indication that he was in one of his sunnier moods. "It feels great! Listen, I can hardly wait for you to hear 'Shelter from the Storm.' I've been working on it like a demon! Too bad you can't hear it with the amps and the whole band," he said, more regretful than annoyed. "I thought for tonight it was best if I played it on my acoustic guitar." He grinned winningly. "I figured your folks weren't ready for ear-shattering electric music to invade their living room."

"I think you're right." I chuckled at the image of the four adults in the other room sitting through a heavy metal rock concert. "Come on in and meet my aunt and uncle."

Puffed out with pride, I made the introductions. Then I went straight to the kitchen to get Skip a Coke and to pour more wine for the others. When I came back, Mary was listening with an expression of intense interest as Skip finished telling her why the Rolling Stones were such geniuses.

"Boy," he was saying, "if I could ever play guitar like Keith Richards, I'd be a happy man! The Stones deserve to be called the best band in the world."

"I must be getting old," Mary said, giving an exaggerated sigh. "They're too loud for my taste these days."

The beginnings of a scowl flicked on Skip's face. "But you don't hate all rock music, do you?" he asked.

"Oh, not at all. We just prefer the mellower stuff. Give us Billy Joel or James Taylor any day!"

"Then you'll like our song," Skip insisted arrogantly, sounding so sure of himself I fidgeted in embarrassment. He must have thought I was uncomfortable at being left out, because he winked at me and added, "It's not just the music that's good, either. Laurie's lyrics can stand with the best of ballads."

"We're certainly eager to hear your song," Mary quickly assured him, ignoring Skip's know-it-all attitude. "We've always thought Laurie was a very talented poet."

"Poet!" Skip turned to me and gave me a look of horror, as if I'd just been accused of being an ax murderer. "You told me you used to write poems when you were a kid. You're not still writing that garbage, are you?"

"Oh—um—I like writing songs more," I blustered. Through the corner of my eye I saw Mary's look of disappointment. She knew I was lying to please Skip, even if it meant denying caring about what I loved most. I felt like a real traitor—to myself. "But that doesn't mean I think poetry is garbage," I added lamely in an attempt not to sell out completely.

There was a big hush after that, and I knew everyone felt uncomfortable.

"Let's eat!" Mom piped up in that kind of overly chipper voice people use when they want to get everybody's attention away from an ugly situation. "The turkey's ready for carving, and I'm starving, to make a very bad rhyme of my own!"

I'll never be able to pay my mother back for the relief I felt as everyone laughed. Her corny joke had done the trick. The atmosphere of the room lightened immediately as everybody stood up and headed toward the dining room.

"I'll help you bring the food to the table, Mom." I went through the swinging door to the kitchen, needing a little time to collect myself. This wasn't working out at all! I was beginning to get the impression that Mary hadn't been won over by Skip. Was it my imagination, or was she casting little searching glances at me when she thought I wasn't looking, as if checking to make sure I hadn't taken leave of my senses? And what about Skip? Had he always been so shallow and argumentative?

Quickly I grabbed a pot of potatoes and poured them into a bowl as soon as Mom came in, so there'd be no chance for us to talk. Then I darted into the dining room to drop them off before coming back to pick up the vegetables. Maybe, I hoped, Skip would be less cranky when he had some food in his stomach—and maybe Mom's delicious dinner would settle the butterflies in mine.

Dinner went off okay. Dad started talking to Don about the new project he was working on, and Mary talked about the work she'd finished on the baby's room and the needlepoint cushions she was making. Skip didn't seem to have anything to say, and I was content to be quiet myself, enjoying the peace and relaxed atmosphere. By the time Mom had poured coffee and served the apple pie she'd baked that afternoon, that earlier strained feeling was completely gone, and I felt happy again and as adoring of Skip as ever.

"Don't worry about the dishes, Laurie," Mom told me when we'd finished with dessert. "We can clear up later. I think we're all waiting to hear your song, so why don't we go back to the living room so Skip can give us his one-man concert?"

She smiled at Skip, giving him silent support, then put her arm around my shoulders as we walked through the hall to the other room. Skip followed us, standing back politely to let the grown-ups go first and stopping along the way to grab his guitar case off the hall table. Mom was being such an angel I couldn't believe I'd ever found fault with her or thought she was old-fashioned and too sure of herself to understand me.

The tune Skip had written was pretty much like the one he'd sung to me when I'd first shown him "Shelter in the Storm." I was touched and proud to hear my words sounding meaningful and loving as Skip sang them in a clear voice ringing with emotion. But the funny thing was, I didn't feel nearly as proud of Skip as I'd thought I would now that I was showing him off. Instead, I felt more proud than ever of my parents and my aunt and uncle as they sat listening with rapt attention, sending pleased smiles my way every now and then.

"Beautiful!" Mary said enthusiastically when Skip had finished and everyone's loud applause had died down.

"You two make quite a team," Don agreed.

Dad came over and hugged me, and Mom, maybe noticing that Skip was looking shy and out of place, was quick to come to the rescue again by praising him. "That's a lovely melody you've written," she told him warmly. "We're pleased you liked Laurie's work enough to spend your time on it."

"Oh, it was nothing, Mrs. Adams," Skip said gruffly, but I could tell by his nervous fretting of the guitar strings that he was flattered.

Everyone insisted Skip sing the song one more time, and they showered more praise on us when he'd finished the encore. "I'm glad everyone likes it. It's not much like the Rolling Stones, is it?" he said kiddingly to Aunt Mary, but I thought he sounded a little as if he was daring her to disagree underneath his light tones.

"It was just the kind of music I like," Aunt Mary said pleasantly, "and it was very nice to meet you at last."

That was that. Skip thanked my mother for dinner, then shook hands with everyone, very dignified and mature. I walked him to the door.

"Mmnnn, I've been wanting to do this for days," he murmured, grabbing me and kissing me so hard little shivers went down my spine.

"Me, too!" I said shakily when he finally let me go.

"You liked the song?" he asked. From the lazy way he was leaning against the hall table, I could tell he wouldn't have believed me if I'd said no.

"With those great lyrics, how could I help but love it?" I laughed. "And the music wasn't so bad, either."

He shrank back in mock terror. "Pulleeze! I don't want all this praise to go to my head! A few kind words of adoration will do."

"Silly!" I laughed again, snuggling close to him, my heart lighter than it had been for days. "I'm glad you liked Don and Mary."

He seemed puzzled for an instant, then said, "Oh, your aunt and uncle." He shrugged. "Yeah, they seem okay. A little square, but what can you expect of people that old?"

"Square? They're not the least bit square, Skip! And I'd never call them old."

"Hey, I said they're okay, didn't I? Look, I'd better get a move on, or I'll be back in full-time quarantine again." He paused for a minute, then said slowly, as if it took an effort, "Listen,

Laurie, I heard you've been hanging out with Jeff Aldridge at the Hut lately. I know I have no right to tell you what to do, but I'd appreciate if you'd stay away from him. That guy's a creep."

"He is not," I said, my voice hot as, surprisingly, I rose to Jeff's defense. "And I haven't been hanging out with him. Yeah, I've gone to the Hut but just with Didi. I can't help it if he comes over and talks to me, can I? It's not as if he's ever asked me out or anything like that."

"Oh, he'd never do *that*," Skip said, laughing scornfully.

"What makes you so sure of that? Is it that you think a smart guy like Jeff couldn't be interested in someone stupid like me?" My voice cracked with hurt. Skip was hinting at exactly what had been worrying me.

"Don't get excited, babe. I didn't mean that. As a matter of fact," he went on, smiling slyly, "I *know* he's interested in you. He told me that first day he saw you in school. And that's why I know he wouldn't ask you out."

"What do you mean?" I asked, puzzled.

Skip leered in triumph. "I told him that I had first dibs on you and that he'd better keep his hands off."

"You what?"

"Hey, I wasn't going to let that conceited quiz kid get to you first." He laughed nastily. "Boy, he would have just loved to say he was dating a chick Reardon had his eye on. Anyway," he finished matter-of-factly, "everything's worked out all right, so it was no big deal, right? We're going steady now, aren't we?"

"Of course," I murmured. But when he was gone, I was left with an unpleasant feeling. There was something dishonest and scheming about Skip telling Jeff he was going with me when he wasn't. The more I thought about it, the more upset I got. On top of it all, he'd put an idea in my head I liked even less. What if Skip's reason for flirting with me and coming on so strong had nothing to do with his liking me for myself? What if he'd gotten me to fall for him just so he could have the pleasure of keeping me from Jeff?

With a heavy heart, I slipped into the dining room and started clearing off the table. Suddenly I didn't feel like being part of the laughter and animated voices I could hear coming from the living room. I just wanted the evening to end as soon as possible.

Chapter Fifteen

I wasn't going to be let off the hook so easily, though. I'd been in the kitchen only a few minutes when Mary joined me. "You shouldn't be out here working all by yourself, Laurie!" she scolded. "Let me help."

"Oh, no, I can do it," I insisted. "Really, you should rest."

"Don't be silly," she said lightly. "There's still

some life in this old girl. You rinse and I'll stack."

I opened my mouth to protest, but she cut me off with a severe look. "I insist, Laurie." She smiled. "I promise I won't get in the way."

She seemed content to scrape the dishes when I brought them in from the dining room, but I noticed that she was also whistling off-key and fidgeting. I was willing to bet she was just biding her time to start talking to me.

I was right. When we were standing side by side, me by the sink and her by the open dishwasher, she said in that kind of casual voice that wasn't really casual at all, "So that's Skip!"

"Ummm." I focused my attention on the plate I was rinsing.

"He's very cute."

"I think so," I said, wishing she'd take the hint that I didn't feel like talking.

"Gee, I should think you'd be dying to tell me all about him," she said stubbornly. Then she added pointedly, "Or at least ask me what I thought of him."

"What do you think of him?" I asked in a tiny voice.

She laughed softly. "Don't sound so threatened, Laurie! You sound as if you're waiting for me to call him names or tell you I hated him."

"You did like him, didn't you?" I asked breathlessly, momentarily forgetting the dirty dishes. "Everyone likes Skip. They just can't help it," I babbled. "After all, he's adorable and talented and tall and funny and—"

"Hold on a minute! Who are you trying to convince? Me or you?"

"W-what do you mean?" I asked. "I don't have to convince anyone that Skip's a prize catch."

"As the great playwright and poet Shakespeare said," she said, putting heavy stress on the word poet as if to remind me that I'd denied being one, "'methinks the lady doth protest too much.' Why do you feel compelled to reel off Skip's good points? Afraid I might have overlooked them? Or is it that you like him more because he's a prize catch than for who and what he really is?"

I might have been able to scoff at her words if she hadn't been looking at me with such affection and concern. But even as she spoke, I heard the words that were already in my heart, "Oh, Mary, I just don't know any more!" I wailed, literally throwing in the sponge and perching miserably on a stool at the breakfast bar, my head in my hands. "I'm so mixed up."

She sat down on the stool next to me and waited until I looked up and met her gaze. "Don't you think you'd feel better if you talked about it? I have a feeling the answers to everything that's bothering you are already there," she said, pointing to my chest. "Maybe they'll come to the surface if you give them a chance."

So I poured out my heart, telling Mary everything: how worried I'd been that I'd go through high school with no dates, how I'd let my whole life revolve around clothes and makeup and boyfriends so people wouldn't think I was a grind, how my grades had slipped, how I didn't seem able to cope with all the new things that were going on in my life.

I didn't keep anything back. I even told her about meeting Jeff and about Skip's confession tonight that he'd lied to Jeff to keep him from asking me out and about Skip's flunking his math test in spite of Jeff's tutoring and about how Jeff had dismissed me as a birdbrain because of the way I'd acted.

"The worst part is that now I'll never be sure if Skip really cares for me or not!" I finished up. "What'll I do if I find out he acted interested in me just to get even with Jeff?"

"Maybe you should tell me a little more about your feelings for Skip instead of what you're afraid he may or may not feel for you," Mary said calmly when I'd finished.

"What do you mean?"

"Well," she said slowly, seeming to choose her words with care, "you've been talking nonstop for fifteen minutes, and I haven't heard you say one word about how you really feel about him. You say he's this and he's that—he's popular, he's cute. But you're not saying, 'I like Skip because he's *this* way.'"

"What did you really think of Skip, Mary?" I asked seriously. "I really want to know."

She took a deep breath. "I thought he was nice enough. A little immature and hotheaded but basically decent. But"—she hesitated—"to be perfectly honest, Laurie, I can't figure out what you see in him. You've never struck me as the kind of girl who'd give her soul to rock music. It seems as if you've given up all your other interests for Skip. Your mother tells me you didn't even go out for Glee Club this year."

"I didn't. Skip thinks Glee Club's silly," I confessed, hanging my head in shame. "I wanted him to like me so badly, Mary, and to keep on liking me! I did everything I thought he'd want me to do. But what good is it doing me? My average is down to a C-plus, I'm so worn out I can barely think, and I'll probably end up with no boyfriend anyway! What a fool I am."

"Oh, Laurie," she said softly, reaching over to wipe the tears trickling down my cheeks, "it's not that bad. And I don't think you're a fool. I think you're a perfectly normal going-on-sixteen-year-old girl.

"When I was your age, my head certainly would have spun if someone like Skip had come along. And believe me, I wasted plenty of time myself fooling around with makeup and hair styles." She giggled. "Would you believe that for six whole months I got up at dawn to iron my hair because straight hair was the 'in' thing? That's all part of growing up. The important thing, though, is that you mustn't ever forget who you really are."

"But I don't know who I am any more," I cried. "I don't know if I'm the old Laurie or the new Laurie. Maybe I'm not anybody any more!"

"Of course you're somebody," she said briskly. "Why do you have to be either the old Laurie or the new Laurie when neither one of them makes you happy? Why not be the *real* Laurie? The Laurie who loves to read and write poetry and who cares about her grades, as well as the

Laurie who cares about how she looks and who feels more attractive and sure of herself? You know, you can care about your grades and your appearance without devoting your entire life to either one. Don't be so hard on yourself."

"Maybe you're right," I said thoughtfully.

"And what about Skip?" she asked softly. "Do you really enjoy being with him all that much?"

I thought it over for a long time, then reluctantly shook my head. "Sometimes, yes, but as a steady thing I guess I really don't. I mean, Skip's all right, but—"

"But?"

"But a lot of the time I find him really boring. I get so sick and tired of just talking about music and having to listen to him putting down anything academic. It just seems so childish!"

Would you believe I felt a thousand times better after I'd admitted that? No wonder I had felt so strained lately, I thought, keeping all those feelings bottled up even from myself. "You're right," I admitted sheepishly. "I've been so busy trying to keep Skip interested in me, I never allowed myself to wonder whether or not I was really interested in him!" Then something else struck me, and my rising spirits took a quick nose dive. "But I've already blown it!" I groaned. "Jeff Aldridge can't stand me!"

"And you'd like him to like you?" she prodded.

I sighed. "Yes, I think I would. I think I've really liked him from the start. I probably would have realized it if I hadn't been so busy trying to win Skip so I could show him off like a trophy and impress everyone else. I don't blame Jeff for thinking I'm a moron."

"If he's as sensitive and sweet as he sounds, I'm sure he doesn't think that at all, Laurie."

"But what can I do, Mary? I can't just go up to him and say: 'The Laurie Adams you think you know is a fraud. Let me show you what a neat person I really am.' Then he'd think I was crazy as well as stupid."

She laughed, and I laughed along with her. "Maybe I *am* crazy."

"No one ever said there's anything wrong with being a little bit loony. Goodness, wouldn't life be dull if everybody was always sane and mature and proper all the time?" She paused, and when she went on, her voice was serious again. "Why not just be yourself? You can't lose that way. Be honest with Skip and give him the chance to find a girl who's genuinely interested in him. And give Jeff a chance to get to know the real you. If he likes what he sees and knows you're not attached, he'll ask you out. If not, you'll still be better off, because you'll know the next boy who does fall for you will like you for who you are."

"Oh, Mary, what would I ever do without you?" I threw my arms around her and hugged her so tightly we both almost toppled off our stools.

"I think you'll do just fine on your own, Laurie," she told me. "Why, look how much you've grown up already!"

There was a sharp rap on the kitchen door,

and Mom stuck her head in. "Are you girls going to chew the fat all night or come out and watch TV with us? There's a wonderful old Fred Astaire and Ginger Rogers movie on in ten minutes."

"Just what I need." Mary jumped up, clapping her hands like a kid on Christmas morning. "Especially now that I've had to hang up my own dancing shoes for a while! C'mon, Laurie," she said, linking her arm through mine and pulling me toward the door. "Now that we've settled all the great problems of the world, I think we deserve to be entertained, don't you?"

"I sure do!" I said with such enthusiasm that even Mom grinned.

That night marked a turning point in my life. All the gloom I'd been immersed in for weeks had suddenly cleared away, and I knew I could never go back to being either the bookworm or the glamour girl again. Mary had helped me see what I'd known deep down inside all along: I was both Lauries now, and any boy who liked me had to like both of them, too.

It was hard for me to break off with Skip, especially when I knew he was depressed, but it wouldn't have been fair of me to put it off.

I told him how I felt when I met him the next day at school. I didn't tell him everything, of course. I wanted to be free again, but I had no desire to hurt him in any way. So I just explained that I thought we should stop seeing each other for a while. "For one thing, I think we're both too young to be tied down," I reasoned. "And for another, I happen to be worried about my own grades. I know you don't think much of grades, but it's always mattered to me to do well in school, and I don't want to stop now. I've discovered that I can't sit in the Hut all the time, listen to all the latest records, write songs, *and* get decent grades. Maybe some people can, but not me."

To my surprise, Skip looked almost relieved. "Maybe you're right, Laurie," he admitted. "I've done some thinking myself since I got grounded, and maybe my dad isn't so off the wall after all. I still think he takes things too seriously, but being benched has made me see how much I like to play football." He smiled a little sadly as he admitted defeat. "Not to mention that I don't want to end up working in a gas station for the rest of my life. It was always easy for me to mock kids who wanted to go to college, but I guess I'd always taken it for granted that I'd get into some school somehow."

He let out a harsh sigh and seemed to have trouble finding his next words. "Don't tell anybody this, please, Laurie. But the reason I was so sure I was going to get an A on the next math test was that I was planning to cheat. I'd decided that's what I'd do, to show Jeff and the coach and my old man. But it dawned on me that if I got caught, I'd probably get kicked off the team, and I'd blow my chance of getting into a decent school."

"But I thought school didn't matter if you were going to be a rock musician," I reminded him.

"It probably doesn't," he said with a touch of

his old defensiveness. "But with the music business the way it is today, everything helps. More and more rock musicians have courses in theory, harmony, and composition behind them, and if I can get into school, there's no reason my dad shouldn't let me choose my own major."

I knew now I wasn't in love with Skip, but talking to him, I found myself genuinely liking him a lot. He was just so much nicer being himself than showing off or trying to act big. Just like me.

"You're not mad about our not going steady?"

"It doesn't seem as if either of us is ready, does it?" He grinned crookedly. "Not to mention that I won't have much time for going out if I'm going to keep my band together *and* pass all my tests."

I walked away from our talk feeling a little shaky but good about myself. It was scary going back into the world as Laurie Adams again instead of as Skip Reardon's girl, but I knew I had to do it, even if some kids dropped me as a result.

It wasn't until I got home that afternoon that I realized I'd stopped worrying about whether Skip had liked me for myself or not. It didn't seem very important any more. I didn't doubt we'd dated each other for all the wrong reasons. But, I reflected, no great damage had been done. In fact, Skip and I had ended up better off than we'd started—we were finally friends.

Chapter Sixteen

Those first few weeks after splitting up with Skip weren't easy for me. Some of my new "friends," the ones who'd called out hellos in the corridors or called me over to their tables to chat at the Hut, started acting like they'd never seen me before. More than once I overheard a girl whispering cattily to another that I'd been "dumped on by Skip Reardon." But I held my head high through all of it.

Thank goodness, my girlfriends stuck by me through it all. Didi, Terri, and Deborah were as warm as ever and, to my amazement, each one of them took me aside to tell me in private they'd never known what I'd seen in Skip! As Didi said, "He's darling, but I just couldn't see you with a guy who never read anything but songs, Laurie. I was sure you'd get bored with him sooner or later."

Imagine that! It just shows how wrong I was about what went on in other people's minds.

I didn't have much chance to go to the Hut before the term ended. I hadn't been exaggerating when I told Skip I had a lot of catching up to do. To raise my grades, I couldn't even afford to get any B's, and that meant studying twice as hard and reviewing all the material I'd skipped over at the beginning of the semester.

The couple of times I did stop in at the Hut with Didi or the other girls, I'd talk to Skip, but I was careful to make it clear to anybody who might be watching that we were friends and nothing more.

Still, I couldn't help breaking into a cold sweat whenever I saw Jeff Aldridge. But I'd learned my lesson with him, too. No longer did I try to impress him by telling him what I'd read or how much I was studying. I was still embarrassed that I'd done that in the first place.

Instead, I did my best to be open and friendly and *not* to flirt or act silly. The more I got to know about him, the more I liked him. I discovered that he wasn't a grind at all, and that, if anything, he had more outside interests than Skip had ever had. He loved reading mysteries and thrillers as much as I did, and in addition to playing the piano, he liked tennis and surfing and had been a lifeguard at the community pool during the summer.

But, as time passed, I became more and more convinced that Jeff wasn't the slightest bit interested in dating me—if he ever had been. Oh, he was friendly, but he made no move to ask me out. I was too proud to hint around or suggest we get together, but not too proud to admit to myself that it hurt. Even though I never saw him with a girl, I decided he must have a girlfriend somewhere and that there was no hope for me. That was life, I told myself, feeling very grown up. No one got everything wanted.

The security of what I'd come to accept as my genuine popularity made my failure with Jeff easier to bear. I began looking forward to going to school every day, and now that I'd caught up on my studies, I found I had more time to join in extracurricular activities. I even sought out the teacher in charge of the Glee Club, and instead of taking the easy way out and telling her I'd been sick when they were holding tryouts, I told the truth, explaining that I hadn't bothered to audition at the time and was regretting it now. She gave me extra proof that honesty is the best policy because she went out of her way to set up a special tryout for me. Mom was as thrilled as I was the day I came home and told her I'd been accepted.

Best of all, now that I wasn't spending all my time mooning about whether or not kids liked me, I became friends with Anna Certowski again. I'd never been proud of the way I'd dropped her just because I'd been afraid she was socially unacceptable. I decided that if she still wanted to be friends with me—and I'd have understood if she didn't—it was too bad if other people didn't like it.

Anna was, well, what my mother would have called "gracious" about it all. The first time I suggested we get together after school to study, she acted like we'd been buddies all along. This time I didn't think her eagerness to be with me was pathetic. I just felt glad that she liked me.

Then, just a week before my sixteenth birthday, we had the final assembly of the semester. It was *the* important all-school assembly, the one at which the honor roll was announced and the kids whose names were called went up on stage to accept a certificate of merit.

That morning I dressed up, not because I expected my name to be read off, but because everybody dressed for the honors assembly. I wore my good navy skirt and navy ballet slippers and the navy and white flannel blazer I'd bought with the money I would have splurged on record albums a month before.

"My, my, don't we look elegant." Dad peered at me approvingly over the top of his paper, and I knew I looked all right if even he'd noticed. "What's the occasion?"

"Honors assembly," I said, spooning sugar over my cereal. "Don't get excited," I added, seeing the expectant smile rising to both his and Mom's lips. "I don't think I made the honor roll."

"Don't worry, Laurie," Mom said kindly, "we don't expect you to be perfect, you know. As long as your grades are decent and you're happy, we're satisfied."

"Did I ever tell you I think I've got the neatest parents in the world?" I asked, grinning from ear to ear as their jaws dropped open. "I know I never say much and that sometimes I don't act as if I think so, but I do."

"Well, we're pretty happy with you, too," dad said gruffly. Mom blinked real fast like she had something in her eye.

I kissed them both goodbye, then hurried out the door. I'd have given anything to have my name on the honor roll, but I couldn't lay the blame on anyone but myself if I didn't. In any event, I knew that next semester I wasn't taking any chances. I'd hear the principal call out Laurie Adams loud and clear then, because I was determined to study harder than I ever had before.

Didi was as dressed up as I was, but she was wearing a frown instead of a grin. "Is something wrong?" I asked as we walked in the direction of the bus stop. "You don't look too happy."

"Why should I be happy?" she asked. She looked close to tears.

"Why not?" I asked, shaking my head in surprise. "You're pretty, you're popular, and you've got Barry Knox. Everybody knows it's only a matter of time before he asks you to go steady." I gasped. "Didi, you two haven't had a fight, have you?"

She shook her head. "No, nothing like that. It's just that Barry's going to make the honor roll, and I'm not. I'm afraid he'll be ashamed to be seen with someone stupid like me."

"Now you sound as bad as I did when I was seeing Skip," I chided her. "Barry couldn't possibly think you were stupid, you dummy," I teased her, trying to make her smile. "If he asks why you didn't get called up on stage, why not just tell him the truth? That you let being in senior high go to your head and goofed off the first half of the semester. I don't think I'm going to hear my name, either, and it's not the end of the world to me."

"Really? You don't care?" She sounded as if she didn't believe me.

"Sure I care—more than I would have admitted in October. But it's the price I've got to pay for all I learned this semester."

She still wasn't smiling, but at least she didn't look as upset. "That's true, isn't it? We *have* learned an awful lot." She sighed as we joined the other kids waiting for the bus. "Gosh, Laurie, why didn't anyone tell us sophomore year was going to be such a chore?"

"Do you think we'd have listened?" I asked. This time, I got an answering grin.

I was already sitting in assembly, between Didi and Terri, when I spotted Jeff walking down the aisle to a seat on the other side of the room. Suddenly I didn't feel so cheerful. He looked so handsome and so *nice* in his blue suit and shirt and tie that my heart just ached. I couldn't forget that maybe I'd have been his girl if I hadn't acted the way I had. I knew I'd eventually get over it, but for the time being it was the hardest part of the lesson I'd learned.

"Doesn't Barry look great in a suit?" Didi whispered behind her hand as he walked in with a couple of other guys. Almost as if he'd heard her from thirty feet away, he suddenly turned and gave her a special smile. Suddenly I felt so alone. How could Didi be depressed about not making the honor roll when she had a boy who cared about her so much?

Then the lights dimmed, the orchestra started

the school anthem, as we all stood. The honors assembly had begun.

They called seniors first, and farther down the row, I could see Janie's chin go up proudly as Bob Elkins' name was called and he strode up the aisle. Soon, I had no doubt, Janie would be hearing her own name.

When the junior list was read off, I waited expectantly to hear Jeff's name, and when it was announced, I almost started to clap. He truly deserved the recognition, I thought proudly. As I watched him walk to the stage, his head held high and a little smile of happiness on his lips, I wondered if Skip was sitting someplace feeling resentful now. I didn't think so. Every time I'd seen him talking to Jeff since the math test fiasco had been settled, it had been plain to see the respect and wish for Jeff's approval on his face. In a funny way, Jeff was the one responsible for both of us deciding to shape up.

Mr. Seefer, our principal, finished reeling off the list of juniors, and I braced myself, setting my lips in a smile, vowing not to look crushed or disappointed.

I was working so hard at not expecting to hear my name that when it was called, right after Dennis Abernathy, I just sat there.

"Go on, Laurie!" Didi nudged me, grinning from ear to ear. "Get up there!"

"I can't believe it," I murmured dazedly, somehow pulling myself to my feet.

Then I was walking up the aisle to the stage, still stunned. But now my smile was heartfelt. When Mr. Seefer handed me my certificate, I managed to thank him. Then, as I took my place with the rest of the honor roll students behind him, I looked down at the piece of parchment in my trembling fingers and saw that it was true. My name was there, in careful black script, along with my semester average, a B+. My studying hadn't been in vain!

Jeff was somewhere behind me, so I couldn't see him while we were all grouped on the stage. Had he even noticed my name being called? I wondered. Had he been pleased to see me walk to the front of the auditorium to accept my honors certificate—or had he just not cared?

I found out the answer to those questions after we'd left the auditorium.

"Congratulations, Laurie!" Didi hugged me warmly when we were out in the corridor. "See? I knew you'd make it!"

"I nearly fainted when I heard my name being read off," I admitted, giggling with relief.

"Good thing you had me there to nudge you, huh?"

I remembered then that this hadn't been a wonderful occasion for everyone. "Oh, Didi, I'm sorry you didn't make it this time," I told her, expecting her to be upset.

But she looked in much better spirits than she had earlier this morning. "No, what you said was right. I'll just have to work harder to make sure my grades are better next term."

"Here comes Barry," I said, catching sight of him over her shoulder. "And from the way he's smiling, I don't think he's upset with you at all."

"Congratulations, Laurie," Barry said politely, his own certificate still clutched in his hand.

I said the same to him, then wandered off so Didi could be alone with him. His arm was around her shoulders, and he was already whispering into her ear as I slipped away. I could tell everything was okay between them. He liked Didi whether she made the honor roll or not. But come spring, I knew her name would be one of those announced by Mr. Seefer at that honors assembly.

"Hey, Laurie, glad to hear you've kept your grades up." It was Jeff. He gave me a shy little smile. "I guess I owe you a double apology for thinking you were just scraping by."

A snappy reply rose to my lips, but I stopped myself from uttering it. "Thanks, Jeff," I said instead. "But you were right at the time. My grades were pretty bad." I held up the piece of paper in my hand. "I wouldn't have this right now if I hadn't started knocking myself out to catch up. I guess I've got you to thank for it. If you hadn't said those things to me, I might never have stopped and thought about how I was doing."

His smile widened, and I thought he looked pleased that I'd flattered him. But they weren't empty words. He really had been a major force in my buckling down. My Aunt Mary was right. Even if Jeff never asked me out, I wouldn't regret having changed my life because of him.

"Listen, Laurie," he began, his voice low and serious, "now that football season's over, I've got more free time, and I wondered—well, would you like to go to the movies Friday night?"

I didn't bother trying to hide my happiness. "I'd love to, Jeff," I told him, a grin on my face nothing in the world could wipe off. "I'd really love to."

"Really?" He looked a little surprised. "You know, I wanted to ask you before, but I was afraid you really hated me."

"I never hated you, Jeff," I said, adding guiltily, "even though I admit I probably acted like I did. But that was a long time ago."

He didn't have anything to say to that, so we just stood there smiling at each other until the bell rang a few seconds later. Then I scrawled my phone number on a piece of notebook paper and floated off to my locker to get my books and go to class.

That was three months ago. Jeff and I are still dating, and, everyone—even Mary—says we make the perfect couple. But we aren't going steady, and we aren't spending all our time together. Jeff has his job, and we've both got plenty of homework to do and outside activities of our own. But this time, I'm certain I've found the right guy, someone who knows what he wants and is grown up enough to see that other kids judge you on more than looks and clothes.

What more could any girl ask for? I celebrated my sixteenth birthday with a brand-new boyfriend—and I didn't miss Skip at all. Jeff even gave me a present I'd been longing for—a thick volume of Shakespeare's plays. Now, can you imagine me asking Skip for something like that?

Not that Skip's the old Skip anymore, either. In just a few months, the change in him is already plain to see. He still talks about rock music all the time, but he has a more serious look about him, and I've spotted him more in the library than in the Hut.

One of the best things that's happened is that I've become a godmother to Mary and Don's absolutely beautiful baby girl, Melissa Diane. Since the night we had that heart-to-heart in the kitchen, Mary and I have been better friends than ever. I know I won't forget everyone who stuck by me during the period I turned into Loony Laurie.

But if I hadn't become *that* Laurie, I wouldn't be the Laurie I am now. I still care about my wardrobe and my makeup—but it's no longer the most important thing in my life. Sometimes I get up a little earlier to put electric rollers in my hair, but more often than not, I don't. I certainly don't feel as if I can't face school these days if I haven't done my hair or spent an hour on my makeup. My makeup or hairdo isn't what makes me who I am.

If that all isn't wonderful enough, Didi and I have ended up being better friends than ever before. You know, neither of us can believe how far out we'd gotten in those couple of months. It's as if we both turned into different people for a little while, people who sometimes weren't very nice to each other. But, even though nei-

ther of us has put it into words, I think we both
accept that we acted the way we did because we
were so desperate to fit in and be liked. I guess
being in too much of a hurry to grow up can
just make you more of a baby than ever if you
let it. I have a feeling it's going to be a long time
before either of us starts acting smug and superior toward the other again. If we ever do,
that is.

During those couple of months with Skip, I
learned that I really like to write songs. I'm still
writing them, and I've gone back to writing
poetry and have joined a new composition club
that started at school.

Jeff and I have even tried to do some things
together in the music department, him at the
piano plinking out a tune and me with my
notebook, trying to make the lines rhyme. We
just do it for fun, and half the time we end up
convulsed with laughter at the dumb songs we
come up with. But we've actually written a
couple of things we like, too, and when Jeff
plays with the dance band next year—when
he'll have the time—he's going to try to teach
them a couple of our favorites.

I've got one song that Jeff may never see,
which I wrote myself on the guitar Mom and
Dad got me for my birthday. It's a song I wrote
just for me, and it sums up how I feel about
everything. I call it "Laurie's Song."

I know I'm young,
But I'm older than I used to be.
I can do anything;
I'll be the girl I choose to be.

Looking ahead to all that life might bring to me,
Loving a boy who's happy just to sing to me.
It took a long time,
But now I'm where I belong.
And this is Laurie's song.

Just when she had something good of her own, her older sister stepped in, again ...

LITTLE SISTER

Yvonne Greene

Cindy feels she's going to be second-rate all her life. Her older sister Christine has the pretty face, the good body and gets all the cute boys. Cindy just can't win.

Then in study hall Cindy meets Ron, an ex-basketball star who's the best actor in high school. He's just been chosen to play Romeo in the big production of *Romeo and Juliet*. Cindy can't believe that Ron's really interested in *her*, Christine's little sister. But this time it seems she's Number One.

Suddenly, Cindy's hopes for romance and happiness are crushed when Christine is chosen to play the role of Juliet. It seems that Cindy will lose again ... unless she can prove to Ron that she's not second best after all.

0 553 20326 6   65p

Nothing makes a summer special like falling in love ...

P.S. I LOVE YOU

BARBARA CONKLIN

When her father left after the divorce, Mariah lost her sense of family. Now she's lost her special summer, too. Instead of fulfilling her dream to become a writer, Mariah has to help her mother with a house-sitting job in very rich, very snobby Palm Springs. People with a lot of money make Mariah uncomfortable.

Until she meets Paul Strobe, the rich boy next door. Paul's not a snob and doesn't act superior. In fact, his sandy hair and piercing blue eyes break down all Mariah's defenses. With Paul, Palm Springs becomes the most romantic place on Earth.

But Paul has to go into the hospital for some tests and then an operation. He's seriously ill and all his family's money can't help him.

Will Mariah lose Paul, too, just when she's found her first love?

0 553 20323 1   65p

A SELECTED LIST OF
BOOKS PUBLISHED BY CORGI

WHILE EVERY EFFORT IS MADE TO KEEP PRICES LOW, IT IS
SOMETIMES NECESSARY TO INCREASE PRICES AT SHORT NOTICE.
CORGI BOOKS RESERVE THE RIGHT TO SHOW AND CHARGE NEW
RETAIL PRICES ON COVERS WHICH MAY DIFFER FROM THOSE
ADVERTISED IN THE TEXT OR ELSEWHERE.

THE PRICES SHOWN BELOW WERE CORRECT AT THE TIME OF GOING
TO PRESS (JANUARY '82)

*All these books are available at your bookshop or newsagent, or can be ordered direct
from the publisher. Just tick the titles you want and fill in the form below.*

....